CRACKED WHEAT
and Other Stories

CRACKED WHEAT
and Other Stories

Hugh Cook

◤ **MOSAIC PRESS**
OAKVILLE NEW YORK LONDON

Canadian Cataloguing in Publication Data

Cook, Hugh, 1942-
  Cracked wheat & other stories

ISBN 0-88962-266-3 (bound). - ISBN 0-88962-265-5
(pbk.)

I. Title.

PG8555.O64C72 1985   C813'.54   C84-099430-3
PR9199.3.C565C72 1985

Published by Mosaic Press, P.O. Box 1032, Oakville,
Ontario, L6J 5E9, Canada. Offices and warehouse at
1252 Speers Road, Unit 10, Oakville, Ontario, L6L
5N9, Canada.

Published with the assistance of the Canada Council
and the Ontario Arts Council.

ISBN 0-88962-266-3 cloth
ISBN 0-88962-265-5 paper

MOSAIC PRESS:
In the United States:
Flatiron Book Distributors, 175 Fifth Avenue, Suite
814, New York, N.Y. 10010, U.S.A.
In the U.K.:
John Calder (Publishers) Ltd., 18 Brewer Street,
London, W1R 4AS, England.
In New Zealand:
Pilgrims South Press, P.O. Box 5101, Dunedin, New
Zealand.
In Australia:
Bookwise International, 1 Jeanes Street, Beverley,
South Australia 5007, Australia.

The Cover Art is a segment of 'Hurrahing the
Harvest' from the Dordt College art collection; Edgar
Boeve, Artist.

ACKNOWLEDGMENTS

Some of these stories have appeared as follows:

"Exodus" in *Malahat Review*; "A Canadian Education" in *Descant*; "The White Rabbit" in *Wascana Review*; "First Snow" in *NeWest Review*; "Cracked Wheat" in *Antigonish Review*; "Homesickness" in *Pro Rege*; "Pisces" in *For the Time Being*; "Clown" in *Fiddlehead*; and "A Lesson in Dance" in *Vanguard*.

Lines from "Joy to the World" by Hoyt Axton used with permission of Lady Jane Music, Tahoe City, California.

CONTENTS

these stories are for my father and mother
and the rest of that first generation

EXODUS

The first grey light of cloudy daybreak filtered through the white gauze curtains, just enough light to open the eyes of the woman in bed. Again Anton had let her sleep when he got up for work. She moved deep under the covers, drawing up her knees for warmth now that she was alone. Then she thought of the infant in the cradle beside her bed and she knew she would not sleep again until she had looked at it. She bent over, and when she saw the child sleeping she lay back. Ach, she would not sleep anyway. Turning in bed made her feel the pain in her groin, and her lips drew tight. But with the pain she also felt relief that the birth was over and that it had gone well.

I am fearful of this birth, Anton, she had said.

Yet it turned out to be the easiest of the four, and as she thought of it now she felt foolish.

Why are you afraid, Mieke? he had said.

I do not know. Who can explain the feelings a woman has before giving birth.

But she did know. There was the memory of her sister Willi dying in childbirth just four years ago during the war. And she and Anton and the children had been in Canada now only one month, arriving in the dead cold of January, and this was her first birth in this new country. Everything was different from what she had known in Holland. Strange words: *po-ta-to   i-ci-cle   cor-du-roy*. She did not need to say the words over and over for them to sound ridiculous. And strange music on the radio: not songs of the folk, *echt*, but music somehow with a pose, sad songs you were being told to like. And strange buses, creamy yellow and foul-smelling, not like the trams in The Hague. Everything strange, even to the details: doorknobs, matches, diapers. Above all, a strange

11

hospital—what unknown things would they do to her there?

Yes, Anton, I admit that it is irrational, but what else is fear? And does that decrease it, make it easier to live with, simply because you can apply a label to it? Besides, we can't afford the hospital.

Then she had asked Dr. Faber if she could have the baby at home, in her room, as in Holland with Ernst.

No. Absolutely no.

Why? Is something wrong?

No, the baby is in normal position. It is just not necessary. And I will deliver it myself. Trust, Mieke. It will go well.

It had. The labour had been mild and the delivery rapid. Dr. Faber had driven her to the hospital through the snow and a short ten minutes after they had arrived she was wheeled into the delivery room, as if the child had willed to leave the womb, to be born—now.

And she would have to rest, home from the hospital now, with Maryanna here to take care of the house. Was she selfish to desire rest? Or was it really rest she desired? Anton had suggested she should leave her room, not to lock herself in all day, as if by doing so she could shut out the world.

It's a new world, Mieke, he had said, we will have to face it.

.   .   .

As Anton steered his bicycle into the parking lot of the plant he noticed that nights were becoming shorter, the sun well up when he arrived. Nor were the mornings as cold. Soon he would have to pedal through spring rain.

He leaned his bicycle against the white brick of the building and stepped inside. The familiar smell of boiled meat hit his nostrils. The hallway was dark as he walked to the locker room. He was early; as usual, no one else had arrived. He placed his lunch pail on the top shelf of the locker, then sat down on the bench. Slowly he performed his morning ritual: remove the shoes and place them in the bottom of the locker; loosen the tie, unbutton the shirt, and hang them up; unbuckle the belt and slide out of the pants; then put on the white shirt and white pants and white hard hat and black rubber boots; finally, slip on the white apron that by the end of the day would be splotched with blood.

He took his lunch pail and walked through the door into the lunchroom. The bright blue walls greeted him as they did every morning. Baby blue. Against the walls stood the vending machines: chocolate bars, coffee, and soft drinks. He sat down at a green wooden table, took out his thermos, and poured coffee into a red plastic cup. He did not care for the plastic taste; every morning he told himself to take a real cup from home.

The coffee steamed into his face as he blew into it with pursed lips. Every new day still felt strange, not his familiar world. But everyone had treated him well—except for Engel. The heavy German accent: What do you mean you don't want to work on Sundays. Everybody works on Sunday! No exceptions! Just like a petty tyrant. A little Hitler. Then permission had come from the front office and Engel had never let him forget it. Eleven more months he would have to stay to fulfill the year's obligation, but what then? More of the same? Perhaps the egg route with Van Delft's . . .

Noises came from the locker room: benches scraping, shoes dumped into the bottom of a locker, metal doors slamming shut. But the voices were subdued; in the morning the men were always close-tongued, their faces grim. The door opened and the men trickled in.

"Mornin', Dutch."

"How ya doin', Anton."

"C'mon guys, hog time!"

He put away his lunch pail, walked to the time clock, and punched in. Six fifty-nine.

.   .   .

It struck her that with each child her timing had been inopportune. This one too. Eight months before emigrating and she had to become pregnant.

I'm sorry it happened, Anton, but the Lord gives it to us nevertheless. He must have a reason. Yes, I know that it is the worst possible time—should we stay until after it is born?

No, that would mean another year at least, and the papers are all drawn up. We will have to go.

But it made her wonder if the life of the child would be any different from that of the others, for the timing was no better. Two days before Ernst was born Vader had died of stomach cancer, his body wasting away while hers teemed, and Ernst entered the world with a tearing of her flesh that prevented her from going to the funeral. And Anneke, born one year into the War. If they had known how long the Occupation would last would they have had her? Yet, four years later, in that winter of '44, Viktor was born. The day after, Artur Meyer, the Jewish jeweller across the street, had leaped to his death after being chased by *polizei* with yelping dogs. Later, she had opened the heavy velour curtains a crack and had seen the body crumpled on the cobblestones. And not enough wood, even, to make a coffin.

Should we have harboured him, Anton?

No. Our first responsibility is to keep the food supply in Holland rather than letting it go to the Germans.

What kind of a world was it when you had to choose between people and food.

The soldiers had come to the store, their voices strident: *Wir brauchen Eier und Milch!*

Sorry. None is available.

But at night Anton and the others, armed with a chair leg or a piece of lead-filled rubber hose, took their bicycles and picked up milk and cheese from the farms. Then Anton had been arrested and sentenced to concentration camp. He was taken by boat to Rotterdam, but in a moment when the soldiers were not looking a woman had stepped out of the crowd and placed her arm in his as if they were lovers and boldly walked off with him. Then she had given him a bicycle and he rode back to The Hague in the dark.

Why had he been saved? Not all were that fortunate. A number of Anton's youth group had been executed, and on a cold January day she had come upon the handbill tacked to a tree, the list of names surrounded by a black border. *Waarschuwing!*

Was it a world to bring children into?

.   .   .

For two hours the hog carcasses had moved by him, back legs spread apart, hanging stiffly from the overhead rail winding through the plant. Only the head hung loose, dangling from the hog by a layer of skin. The carcasses were bloated, pink and smooth now that the hair had been singed off. They were no longer animals but meat, scalded and clean.

In his left hand he held a hook, in his right a knife. As each hog passed by he sank the hook lightly into the meat behind the jawbone, pulled the head toward him, and cut the meat off the jowls, not all the way but almost, so that it would not fall to the floor. Otherwise Engel would holler at him. Farther down the rail someone else would cut off the jowl. Where the carcass had a blemish he sliced it away, and the body showed a splotch of white fat beneath the pink skin. Between hogs he honed his knife on the hook, always honing, honing, keeping the knife razor sharp. Or he dipped it behind him into the little tub keeping the knife wet so the blood would not dry.

On his right, Walt Kratoska made a long cut down the belly of the carcass so that after it rounded the corner Doug Hamel could make one more slash and pull out the stomach and intestines. The plant was hot, and the men sweated heavily.

They stood on a meshed metal platform that ran below the overhead rail. It was raised two feet above the cement floor so that Barry, the kid with the hot water hose, could keep the floor clean. Everywhere was noise. He could hear the roar of the engines one floor down, the engines that heated the boilers and ran the vats producing blood and bone meal and that turned the waste products into animal food. On his left Les Brown's saw emitted a screaming whine as it cut through the hog's backbone. Metal hooks clanked as the carcasses moved along the rail. And far off to the right, where the women made the sausages, the knives of the chopper rattled in the steel bins, screaking as they hit the meat.

．　　．　　．

She must have been dozing again, for the shrill cries of the child woke her. Yes, twenty after ten! She hated to leave the warmth of the blankets, for she knew the room was cold. She flipped back a corner of the covers, swung her legs gingerly to the floor, and sat a moment on the edge of the bed, marvelling at the child. *Klein mannetje*. Its face was wrinkled and red as it screamed, eyes clenched tight, one hand balled into a fist waving in the air. The mouth opened wide and the lips, thin and dry, curved around the smooth red bridge of the toothless gums, the little white sucking blister pouting from the middle of the upper lip.

She rolled back the cover of the cradle, lifted out the child, and brought it to the commode, where she changed its diaper. The little button of penis still showed blood from the circumcision, and from the navel protruded the crusty stump of the umbilical cord. Then she placed the child on the bed and lay down beside it, balancing herself with her right elbow. With her left hand she unbuttoned the top of her robe and opened it. She pulled down the flap of the nursing bra and, placing her fore and middle fingers on her breast, brought the nipple to the child's mouth. Instantly the screaming stopped, as if turned off by a switch. The child drank hungrily, now and then giving high-pitched croons of contentment.

Strange how they were all the same. So easily within our capacity to please. And what were they anyway? Not so much the mere consequences of our love-making—for who knew when?—as they were our guests. *Geschenken*. Gifts. *My bones were not hidden from thee when I was made in secret, and was stitched together as embroidery in the lowest parts of the earth.*

Embroidery. The cells knit intricately together. Such a weaving of images! And when its time had come, born. Eagerly, rushing to meet its world.

And she?

.   .   .

After what seemed a long time he could finally see the end of the line of hogs, which must mean lunchtime soon, and sure enough there was Barry flushing the floor with the hot water hose, the water turning red with blood, shooting pieces of fat and waste to the drain, steam rising everywhere. Five more hogs. Four. Again, the cutting back the meat, his knife slicing easily. Then he was done, washing the knife in hot water and putting it away with the hook. He wiped the sweat from his brow.

"Hey Dutch, let's go!"

Kratoska and Hamel waited for him, and together they walked to the lunchroom.

"See what the old lady packed me today. Please, I tell her, no more braunschweiger. Like, I only see about three thousand sets of guts a day as it is!"

"Beats havin' to make it yourself. I'm workin' too, the missus says. Either we take turns makin' for both, or make your own. How d'ya like that!"

Anton cut in. "You fellows ever hear what Engel says when he takes visitors by Wilkins and Jacobs? 'Und over heer ve heff two men making chitterlings, a delicacy highly favoured by darkies.' How do you like that!"

They took their lunch pails from the cubicles along the wall and sat at a table. Smoke began to hang in the air. Anton looked out the window and saw that it had begun to rain. *Verdorie*, he would get wet again pedalling home. He'd have to buy a car, that was all there was to it. It had gotten to be too awkward with the distances so much greater here than in Holland. Perhaps if he could put in some overtime on Saturdays for a while, then maybe next month—

"What do you think, Dutch?"

"What—?"

"Walt here says that Engel's turds come out like a string of franks. What do you think?"

"You should not be so worried about Little Hitler. He can't do nothing."

"Whaddya mean, Little Hit—hey, that's good Dutch! Yeah, I like that! Little Hitler!"

"I guess you should know, Anton, you bein' over there and all."

.   .   .

For as she lay back staring at her ceiling, what images, and how they came!

During the War soldiers banged on doors in the middle of the night and took men away in green vans which screamed *ooo-gah ooo-gah*! Anton built a secret compartment beneath the bathroom floor and he had to go in there several times when the soldiers knocked on the door, and the last time he crawled in and she saw him lying there it took every effort of her will to close the trap door and replace the linoleum, for it looked to her as if she was about to close the lid on his coffin.

After that she was willing when he talked to her about emigrating. Four years later their belongings were packed into a shipping crate the size of a small bedroom, all the objects so precious to her that it seemed a part of her was packed with every paper-wrapped cup and saucer, every photograph, every brown velvet chair, the crate slowly filling until with the nailing shut of the last board it seemed her own confinement was complete.

On the pier at Hoek Van Holland, it was difficult to say goodbye with so many tears and embraces. Then she walked up the gangplank, the wooden steps swaying, and she felt she was walking into an ark and would soon see the disappearance of her familiar world. Later, the boat slid away from the dock, the handrail vibrating with the deep churn of the engines, the people diminishing until she saw only the white handkerchiefs waving frantically, growing smaller and smaller until they were mere pinpricks, and then they too disappeared. Then the buildings were gone. An hour later she saw only water behind her, and everything she had known was gone. Ahead of her stretched a blank horizon.

Confined to her cabin, never morning sickness like that seasickness, never so much vomiting, the floor heaving and the drab panelled walls of the cabin swimming without end. Outside, only water, staring back unblinkingly at this mote of a ship. *And there shall be no more sea.* Yes.

Finally they had arrived in Halifax, only to have five more days on the CPR—five whole days and still in the same country! The train rolled through bleak rock in the east, then through barren farmland filled with snow, punctuated by stubble of corn. The prairies stretched endlessly, the snow glinting hard under a pale winter sun. Even inside the train it was cold, and they huddled under blankets, the windows between the cars solid crusts of ice. At night she saw nothing, the blankness broken only by the occasional yard light of a farm, increasing her sense of isolation. Then the mountains—does **anyone** live in this country?—before the train ground into the station in Vancouver with hissing clouds of steam.

God brought us **here**?

.   .   .

He tried not to watch Engel's movements, but despite himself he wanted every moment to know the foreman's whereabouts as he slithered along the plant's wet floors. Just do your job. The man is not that important. Yet he could not get him out of his mind.

One day Engel had him work at the bologna machine with the women. They pushed the lever and the bologna oozed out of the tube, round and red and huge, slowly filling the plastic packing he had placed over the nozzle. Then Engel had come by and had made an obscene comment. Right in front of the women. But get him out of your mind.

Tomorrow was Saturday. Should he ask for overtime, or should he work at home? Perhaps the baby could sleep with Anneke in her room, and he would not have to build the room in the basement yet. Ach, but that was just a stopgap. He'd have to build it eventually. Where would he get the money for the lumber? The door he could get from Dijkstra. Perhaps on his way home he should stop by the building being torn down on Kingsway, and he could get some used lumber. If not for the room, he could always use it for the chicken shed.

Come to think of it, maybe the egg route for Van Delft's wouldn't be such a bad idea after—

"Everything under control, Koning?"

Engel! Where had he come from? The man's face was right next to his, shouting into his ear so that he could smell the nicotine. Sweat broke out on his forehead. He resented the hate in himself, knew it wasn't right, and yet he couldn't help detesting the man. He heard the German accent and he thought of the German soldiers by the store and Artur Meyer and the woman in Rotterdam and the execution of his friends. The hard hat was too much like a helmet, the frock too fastidiously clean, no blood ever touching it. A whited sepulchre.

"Make sure you keep the knife clean, Koning."

"Yes sir."

"And get Barry to clean the platform, not just the floor. We got inspectors around here, you know."

"Yes. **Sir.**"

Not too heavy now, Anton, but the fool! for Engel didn't even catch on:

"And listen, Koning, we're **all** working men here. I get my pay check once a week, just like you do. No rank here. Not like them bastards up in the front office."

But he knew Engel couldn't wait to move up into the front office.

Ask him. No. From him he will not beg. Ask him! You need the money! No. He'd rather starve.

Engel started to turn away and desperately Anton reached out to touch him on the shoulder. "Wait!"

"What you want?"

"Can I work tomorrow?"

"I'll see. I'll let you know later."

.   .   .

Maryanna had taken care of the house since the birth, so that Mieke had been able to rest. She had found strength in her room, in the objects so familiar to her. On the dresser stood the photograph of all the family and friends who came to say goodbye at Hoek Van Holland—except Vader and Willi, whose photographs stood alone. Beside them, her first psalm book, with crinkly pages of onion paper, the notes not round but diamond shaped. The oak linen closet, its front divided into a triptych by two doors and a large mirror, given to her for a wedding present by her parents. And deep within the closet the baptism gown she had made from her wedding dress, the baptism gown worn by Ernst and Anneke and Viktor, its white silk undoubtedly wrinkled. Should she use it for the child? Or would it only bring again the dark events that had surrounded the birth of her other children? Where was the promise of the covenant?

She had talked with Anton about a name.

This one will be named after me, vrouw, he had said. If it is a girl I do not know what we will do, call her Antoinette, I suppose, but Anton will be his name. Every man must have a son who is named after him, and it is right that it be the first one here, for he is a sign of what is to come.

Would he be like his father? Well, he might do worse. Nineteen she was when she had first noticed Anton, he with his blond hair, bristly as a brush, especially when wet. And large ears. Those large ears! She had caught him staring at her during catechism and turning away self-consciously when she looked at him in return. He was on her mind after that, she remembered, while she worked behind the counter at Bovenkamps'. Apparently he had thought of her too, for shortly thereafter had come the letter. The excitement with which she had opened it after taking it to the sanctity of her room! Who's your letter from, Mieke? Huh, Mieke? We didn't know you had a pen pal! Ha ha! The thin blue paper had rustled in her hands. *Lieve* Mieke it said. *Lieve* Mieke, would you like to go together to the youth conference at Leiden? She smiled now at the formality of a written invitation. She had talked about it with friends. Yes, he will ask you, they had said. Any fool can tell that. She had expected a personal conversation, perhaps, or a telephone call, but come to think of it the letter was typical of him. How formal and honourable he had been in everything, although more from shyness and a sense of propriety than from gallantry.

There had not been enough privacy. Too much getting to know each other in their homes with teasing brothers and sisters—Mieke has her first *vrijer*! One Sunday at his house, the next at hers, but despite their lack of time alone their understanding of each other had grown. Then the four year engagement while they tried to save money. And towards the end when they were alone, he always holding back, holding back.

It is no good this way, Anton. There comes a time when love needs to be expressed.

But how shall we then live?

Better than we do now. Now it's like you've been given a present a month before your birthday but you are told not to open it, only carry it around with you. Time to bring on the birthday, Anton, time to open the present.

Time to open the present!

But not before the past had been granted its due and was no more than the past.

·   ·   ·

Again the line of hogs came to an end and he cleaned and put away his hook and knife.

"Barry, will you clean off the platform too?"

He sat down before his locker and slowly pulled off his boots and the apron red with blood and the white pants and shirt, and put on his old suit coat and tie.

"Hey Anton, don't see why you wear the fancy duds to this job. It isn't Sunday every day you know."

"Ja, more than you think!"

. . .

She lay back again staring at her ceiling and remembered her sister Willi having her miscarriage during the War, hemorrhaging in her womb because of the bomb shrapnel in her body, sitting on the toilet and holding a cup to catch the blood, as if it were too sacred just to flush away but ought instead to be saved for sprinkling on some altar. The ambulance had come too late and the sacrifice had indeed been made.

Willi! *Lieve zus!* It was more than you and your child that miscarried. Here was the pattern of the old world! And the new?

Suddenly she realized that the child had been quiet a long time. She leaned out of bed to look, and saw that the child was sleeping on its drawn-up knees like a penitent prostrate before an angry god. How still he lay. Not even the rise and fall of breath. Surely—she leaned over and gave the cradle a bump with her hand but the child gave no flinched reaction. She leaned out further, pain in her groin, and placed her hand against the cheek. It was warm. Yes, for as she looked at the membrane of skin beneath the fleece of hair at the top of his head, the little spot where the skull had not yet formed, she saw the membrane pulse with the throb of blood—pulse—pulse—like a faithful promise. Then she lay back. It was well.

. . .

When he stepped outside, the other men had already left in their cars. The rain had started again, but he didn't mind: tomorrow he could work, Engel said. Tonight he would draw up some plans for the room in the basement. The boys could sleep there.

He wondered how Mieke's day had been.

. . .

She remembered that for the wedding he had worn a black suit and grey top hat, his large ears sticking out underneath. Later, in bed, he had been shy and awkward, she confident and receiving, but afterward she had cried although at the time she had not known why.

How far we have come, we two. How we have had to learn even to make love. Now, with the baby, it had been a long time. But this birth was not difficult, and she would heal soon. It would be good.

She pulled back the cover and eased herself out of bed. She walked to the linen closet and took out the baptism gown, caressing it. It would have to be ironed.

Then she left her room.

A CANADIAN EDUCATION

My father's first glimpse of the Fraser Valley, its loam black like the polder soil of our native Holland, convinced him we had immigrated to the right place. He was a landscaper and an elder in the Dutch Reformed Church, and when increased government bureaucracy after the War made life miserable for the small businessman, not only did every drop of his stubborn Dutch blood rebel at the idea of having to hire himself out to another man, he also found it difficult to render honour to the governing authorities as he was commanded to do by St. Paul, and he felt forced to emigrate. We said farewell to Holland, crossed the Atlantic, and bought a house in the Valley on an acre of land right beside the Fraser River dike. The gravel road the house stood on was rutted by deep potholes that seemed always filled with creamy grey rain water while its edges rose in banks of oval-shaped stones the size of my fist.

The day we moved in, a girl about my age stood at the edge of the road, watching. I wondered where she had come from, for the only other house nearby was a shack that clung to the dike, squatting on a narrow strip of no man's land, and I did not think anyone could possibly live there. The girl watched us all morning, as if she had never seen as odd an assortment of furniture as we carried into the house. In the afternoon I walked over to her. She was a scruffy creature, her brown hair long and unruly like a plant gone to seed, her ragged shirt and brown pedal pushers smeared with river clay. But I must have been equally strange to her in my grey argyle socks and herringbone *drollevangers*, a pair of plus-fours which in Dutch meant "turd-catchers." The girl looked askance at me a long time, circling warily. I understood no English, but no English was needed: the disbelief on the girl's face was eloquent. I motioned for her to follow and walked toward the river, confident I'd find the proper weapon. A rusty spike lying near the shack sufficed. I gouged it into the knee of my pants once, twice, six times, then tore the gouges into a broad rip. "Eddie," I said, pointing at myself. The girl smiled at me like a fellow conspirator. "Aileen," she said.

Gradually I learned English and gradually, accompanied by my new friend Aileen, I began to learn a new world. My classroom was the dike. The neighbouring farmland rose up to it; its brow was grooved by two stony wheel-ruts, formed by farmers' tractors, running parallel through tall grass that left tiny seeds clinging to our legs after a rain, then the ground dropped off to the river in banks of slimy clay. The river slid eternally by, mysterious and grey. Miles downstream where New Westminster and Vancouver dumped raw sewage into the river the water turned an oily brown.

Inspired by the Bible stories my father read at the supper table every day, I taught Aileen war games on the dike. I explained that we were Israelite spies searching out the land of Canaan, hotly pursued by Amalekites, Midianites, Jebusites, and the ten-foot-tall sons of Akan, represented, with a necessary adjustment of the imagination, by our smaller brothers and sisters, and although Aileen understood not the slightest bit of the Bible stories she did enjoy the game. I tried to think of a way we could use the Fraser River as a possible Jordan we could cross with a miraculous parting of the waters, but the river was half a mile wide where we lived, and the feat proved too prodigious for even my imagination.

I also told Aileen my father's stories of the War. We grabbed armfuls of stones from the edge of our road and, pretending they were hand grenades, heaved them round-armed at German submarines in the river, where the stones landed with a deep gurgle and an appropriate explosion of water. We had to make sure my father did not see us removing the stones, for he had a rage to suppress chaos wherever he encountered it in God's creation, and he would rake the stones from the edge of the road into the potholes. Had any other houses been nearby I would have been horribly embarrassed by the sight of my father wielding a garden rake in the middle of a gravel road as if it were a flower bed.

We also fished. Huge log booms lay tied there in the river and we weighted our lines with a heavy metal nut, cast them upstream, and watched them pass by with the current. Of course we hoped to land a coho or sturgeon but all we ever caught were bullheads.

"This'd be a great place for diving," I said, about to jump in.

"No, don't!" Aileen shouted. "The current's too strong."

"Well, we can get around that. What if we tie a rope around our middle."

We ran back to my house, Aileen hanging back at the edge of our property, and I took a long rope from the shed. We brought it back to the log boom and took turns swimming, the water shocking us with its cold even in late summer as we floated on our backs with the current and then fought our way back upstream like spawning salmon while being towed by the person on the other end of the rope. We swam in our clothes and afterward lay on the rough bark of the logs to let the sun dry us out. The back of Aileen's hair came together like a fish's tail and her arms and legs, tanned and wet, glistened like the sleek hide of a sea animal.

One day, however, I noticed mean purple welts on her upper arm. I asked her how she had got them but she said nothing. I asked her again and she became evasive, finally signalling an end to the matter by snapping "Never mind!"

She lived alone in the shack with her father and little brother, her mother having run away several years ago. I did not see her father often, for he seldom came outside. He did not have a job and I would see him now and then at the first of the month when he drove a battered grey De Soto into town to pick up his welfare check.

Their shack was covered with dilapidated wood shingles that seemed long ago to have been painted maroon but now hung grey and naked to the sun and rain. The front door was raised two feet off the ground and had no steps while the back of the house hovered over the river, supported by wooden stilts caked with clay. Parts of cars—transmissions, mufflers, piston rods—lay scattered through the yard like the innards of some huge dismantled animal in grass stained black with dried pools of oil. The place had such an air of squalor that whenever Aileen went in I automatically stayed behind, partly because I knew my presence inside would be an embarrassment to her and partly because I was afraid of what I would see.

Only once did I enter. Aileen and I were walking from the river after a swim when she suddenly yelped and started hopping on one foot, holding the other with her hands.

"What's the matter?" I said.

"Cut my foot on something!"

When we looked blood welled from a gash between her toes.

"You'll have to clean it. Have you got some iodine?"

"I think so." She put her arm around my shoulder and I helped her inside.

The shack seemed to be one large room. I looked for a couch while I waited but did not see one and sat on the edge of one of several beds, covered with rumpled brown blankets, standing in the front of the room. Aileen's father sat opposite me at a table, rolling cigarettes with a machine. He tamped tobacco into a rubber roller, slipped in a long piece of cigarette paper, wetted it with the sharp tip of his tongue, and turned a crank. Out fell a foot-long cigarette which he then cut into three smaller ones with a razor blade. He did not seem at all concerned with Aileen's foot, nor did he speak to me, although he looked at me now and then by raising his eyes but not his head from the little pile of cigarettes on the table. One of his eyes was game, its colour the same creamy grey as the rainwater in the potholes of the road while the other eye, having to do the work of two, seemed doubly piercing. His brown hair fell over his forehead in greasy knives. His mouth was small, as if it had been placed in his face as a hurried afterthought.

At the far end of the room stood a counter with shelves beneath it, a sink, and a wood stove, its black pipes splotched with rust, while from the ceiling dangled three or four coils of brown gummed paper covered with flies. The floor was bare wood; pieces of grey linoleum lay scattered haphazardly about. The room was dark even in the middle of the day and smelled of dirt, urine, and wood smoke. Compared to Aileen's shack, our house was one of order — physical, moral, religious order. My father could not abide sloppiness, neither in a place nor in human action. "Remember, Eddie," he said to me, "life is a flower bed, a garden to be dressed." He believed that every human being had his own predestined place in life, as did every cup and saucer in the cupboard, each rake and shovel in the shed. And so the physical objects in our house took on for me moral pattern and design: on the living room wall, the intricately woven tapestry of a perfectly straight-lined field of tulips; the oak bookcase with glass doors, the books sitting on the shelves like venerable, leather-bound saints: Bible commentaries, Abraham Kuyper's *Gemeene Gratie*, S.G. De Graaf's *Verbondsgeschiedenis*, Josephus's *History of the Jews*, complete with detailed pen-and-ink drawings of the Old Testament, which I studied for hours on rainy days; the pump organ on which my mother played psalms, exotic labels like *melodia*, *dulciana*, and *vox humana* in old Germanic script on its white ivory stops; resting on a wall rack, the white stoneware smoking pipes from Groningen, their graceful stems curved and long — symbols all of the homely object's sanctity, as in a Vermeer, engraved like Zechariah's harness bells with the words "HOLINESS UNTO THE LORD."

But my father also had an earthiness that I found hard to reconcile with this sense of holiness. At the supper table, after he had made sure that I'd left not a particle of potato on my plate, he would read the Bible story, fold his thick fingers in closing prayer, and then light his usual cigarette. Then he would hold out to me his huge forefinger, nicotine-stained and caked with dirt. "Pull it," he would say, and the exact moment I yanked on it he would let a loud fart, laughing hard, while my mother protested, but not without trying to stifle a smile.

He used real manure rather than chemical fertilizers, and occasionally I rode along in the pickup when he drove to a Dutch farmer for a truckload. "Best stuff in God's creation," he said as he swung a shovelful into the truck. Once when the manure lay heaped higher than the sides of the pickup he stuck a daffodil into the top of the steaming mound, and that's how we drove home.

He worked hard those first years to improve our house and yard. The entire inside of the house he remodeled room by room, and we hauled truckloads of old plaster, wood laths, and torn linoleum to the dump. The yard, which before had been splotched with bare spots broken only by broad-leaved weeds with nubbled stems, now sported a lush green lawn. Surrounding the house lay large flower beds filled with Dutch bulbs—crocuses, tulips, hyacinths—for the spring, and evergreen shrubs for the rest of the year. Throughout the yard my father planted apple, pear, and plum trees that later bore so heavily he had to support the branches with two-by-fours.

The improvement of our yard only accentuated, by contrast, the ugliness of the shack on the dike. My father considered it an eyesore in his garden. Aileen and her father must have felt the pressure, as they saw beauty steamrolling towards them, to conform or be pushed back into the river by the onslaught. My father complained to the city council of the illegality of the shack's location but was unsuccessful in bringing about any action. The least next thing he could do, I suppose, was disapprove of my playing with Aileen.

"Can't you play with your own friends?" he asked.

"She **is** my own friend," I said.

"Eddie, you know what your father means," my mother said.

Actually, my parents need not have worried. Aileen attended the public grade school in town and therefore I saw little of her during the school year. I pedalled my bicycle four miles to the Christian school, often through rain, and Aileen's yellow school bus would pass me with a spray of water. By the time we both got home it was late afternoon, the day cold and damp with darkness setting in.

The Christian school stood beside the church. It was a low wooden structure with large windows, and on the days it rained I looked out and felt good about being inside, although at times I thought about my father having to work in the mud. Our principal was Mr. Arkema, who spoke with a thick Frisian accent and whom

we called Arky. "Better watch out, boy, or Arky'll get ya." At
Christmas time we boys all sang *Arky Herald Angels Sing* at the top
of our lungs while trying to keep a straight face, and Mr. Arkema
must have wondered why we loved that particular carol so much.
Our classrooms were panelled with sheets of plywood painted with
a white stain and above the green chalkboard Mr. Arkema had
stapled black cut-out letters that said, "THE FEAR OF THE LORD
IS THE BEGINNING OF WISDOM." Thumbtacked to the side wall
were pictures of John Calvin wearing an odd visored cap with ear
flaps, Martin Luther with a lumpy, florid face, and Ulrich Zwingli,
whose face I cannot recall at all.

Most of the boys at the Christian school came from farms,
raw-boned rough-edged kids whose screams rang raucously over
the playground. As for the girls, there had been one glaring gap in
my moral education, one subject so sacred that my parents never
spoke to me about it, assuming, I suppose, that God himself would
enlighten me when the time came. My time came late. I can recall
that the summer before I graduated from grade eight Aileen once
asked me, "What did the Egyptian man say to the Egyptian woman?"

"I don't know," I said, "what?"

"Come into this pyramid with me and I'll make you a mummy,"
Aileen said, and I snickered as loud as she did.

Even as late as that summer Aileen and I still played on the dike,
and she must have wondered when I would stop seeing life as a
childhood game. But then something happened later that summer
that at once changed my friendship with Aileen.

We had gone to pick wild blackberries along the dike several
miles from where we lived. It was an area more industrial than our
own. Logs lay stacked on top of each other and a sawmill belched a
funnel of black smoke into the sky. Large piles of sawdust lay like
rounded pyramids. The dike there was dotted by small shacks
covered with asphalt shingles or sheets of corrugated tin, and as we
walked by a shack an old man opened the door, pointed a finger at
Aileen, and waved her towards him. He wore a grey undershirt and
a brown pants that hung low on his hips, the belt dangling unbuckled
at his waist. I hesitated, unsure what he might want. The man
smiled and said, "Come here," again waving us towards him.

Then Aileen's voice came to me with an authority I had never
heard in her before. "Keep walking!" she said, and I followed her as
she walked briskly away until we were far from the shack.

"What did he want?" I asked.

"As if you didn't know," Aileen sneered, and as soon as she said it
I did know, and felt silly that I hadn't. My parents' silence meant,

however, that the only word I had for it was one I had seen smeared on the walls of public toilets and had heard from the lips of profane boys. The meaning of the word lay not so much in its denotation as in its sound, beginning with a vicious puff of air held momentarily between sneering lips and teeth, then the brusk vowel, and ending with a brutally hard stop deep in the throat.

Nothing in my past had prepared me for such overt depravity, and it disturbed me that I had not at once recognized it. Equally unsettling, however, was my sudden realization that I would never look at Aileen again in the same way. She knew it too and we walked home not saying a word, the silence between us awkward as between strangers.

The following spring I graduated from the Christian school, and after working with my father during the summer, joined Aileen that September in side-stepping the potholes of our gravel road as we walked to the highway to catch the public school bus. At first I felt awkward walking with her and occasionally I would wait until she had passed by our house, she looking in uncertainly, but since we ended up having to wait together at the bus stop anyway it was impossible for me to avoid her totally, and not walking with her was too obvious a snub. She carried her books with her arms folded across her chest as we walked, speaking little, our lives so distant from each other now.

I did not find her attractive. Other girls, it seemed, had bodies shapely and lissome beneath soft sweaters and rounded skirts that made me dream about them at night, but Aileen wore baggy cotton dresses, her hair was still unruly, and her body, although well-developed, was slouching and graceless. But it was as much an unattractiveness of character as of appearance; she seemed to have no friends, and I would often see her walking by herself between classes.

The high school was an old grey stone building, three stories tall, at the edge of town. The wooden stairs had been worn hollow by students' feet that had shuffled across them since 1919, the date carved in the cornerstone. In the classrooms, blackboards were made of thick slate, while above them, covering walls of sickly green, hung framed pictures of the Queen flanked by John A. Macdonald and Wilfred Laurier on one side, Louis St. Laurent and John Diefenbaker on the other. Our day opened with the homeroom teacher reading a Bible passage selected carefully not to offend any particular faith, then we proceeded to our classes.

Scattered fragments are all I remember from what we learned:
lines from beginners' French (*J 'entre dans la salle de classe. Je
regards autours de moi. Je prends ma place*), taught by a tight-
lipped middle-aged woman who constantly reached a hand into the
shoulder of her dress to straighten a sagging strap, and some boys
reported with great authority that this was because she had only
one breast; lists of countries' exports and imports, taught by an
immigrant from Scotland whose brogue we mimicked so mercilessly
that we drove him to a nervous breakdown midway through the
year; the formula for balancing equations, taught by Mr. Anderson,
whose death in an automobile accident was reported in the *Province*
a year after I graduated. The one teacher who seemed to take a
genuine interest in students was Mr. Charbonneau, who taught
social studies and was boys' counsellor.

More important than my classes were the noon hours I spent with
a few of my Dutch friends. We wolfed down our Gouda cheese
sandwiches while teachers patrolled the aisles, then we went to
Tommy's, a small Chinese grocery, where we bought chocolate
bars and browsed in a large rack of men's magazines. Then it was
three doors down to Snook's, a pool hall where we also spent some
evenings. My parents did not appreciate my going there, for what
they saw through the unpainted top half of the front window as
they drove by was darkness broken by stark cones of smoke-filled
light through which human figures moved hazily, and my parents
were automatically suspicious of any haunt requiring such darkness.
I suppose there may have been some basis for their fears since the
place was frequented by assorted hoods and dropouts, but to me
there was something aesthetic in the expanses of brilliant green felt
and the soft click of billiard balls. Besides, Snook's gave us a place to
smoke.

My father smoked acrid Export non-filters and for a year or two
had been giving me one on New Year's Eve or my birthday, but I
would have to educate my parents about my smoking now. If they
did not like my going to Snook's I would have to smoke openly at
home. Besides, I now spent summers and Saturdays working with
my father, starting early in the morning while the grass was still
sopping wet with dew, and it was often not until six or seven in the
evening before the wheels of my father's pickup finally jounced
homeward through the potholes of our gravel road, and I felt that if
I was old enough to work like a man I was also old enough to smoke
like one. At first I kept the cigarettes in my pants pocket with a
handkerchief covering the package to disguise its telltale shape, but
the emptier the package got the more squished the cigarettes became,

so that it was time for phase two. The package was now moved to my shirt pocket but hidden behind larger pieces of paper so that the yellow edge of my Sportsman's was evident only when I bent forward. After a week or two I began openly carrying the package in my shirt pocket, smoking the occasional cigarette right in the house, and when my parents did not protest I knew I was a man.

By the time I entered grade twelve I had my own social world, which consisted mostly of Saturday night roller skating parties and Sunday evening coffee kletzes with the church's young people. I rarely if ever went to school functions, and saw little of Aileen other than our daily walks to and from the bus. She had become not much more to me than a girl who happened to live next door, and seemed to have little connection with the small girl with whom I had fished and swum.

"I noticed you don't hang around much with Canadian kids," Aileen said to me one day as we walked home. It was October, and ahead of us the yellow leaves of the poplars on the dike fluttered to the earth in a stiff, cold wind.

"I guess I got my own friends," I said. We separated a moment as we walked around opposite sides of a pothole, then we came together again. Her arms held several books against her stomach. She did not wear a coat even in this fall weather, and just looking at her made me even colder. I could see the line of her brassiere coming from around her back and under her arm. She held the books under her breasts.

"You're not missing much anyways," she said.

"What do you mean?"

"Just that there's not much to them. The girls have one thing on their minds, and the guys are all after the same thing."

It was a line that seemed to come straight out of the magazines I browsed in at Tommy's store. But she was right about the guys. They had one-track minds.

"They're just like my father," Aileen said. She did not look at me and I knew she wanted to say more. I waited and after some steps she spoke again. "You want to know something?"

"What."

"I never told you, but did you know he makes me sleep with him?"

I turned to her sharply.

"Who?" I said, "your **father**?"

She nodded. I thought suddenly of the old man in the shack by the sawmill, beckoning her to him with his crooked finger, except this time it was her own father. "You mean—he forces you to?"

"Yes." I was sure she was close to tears.

Blood rose to my temples. "Then you've got to tell somebody! He—he can't do that!"

"He said he'd kill me if I did. So don't tell anyone."

Her voice was flat, unimpassioned, as if stating a fact so unarguably true one might as well acquiesce to it.

We were stopped in front of my house and I did not know what to say. Then Aileen began to walk slowly away and as I saw her rounded shoulders and the hem of her skirt hanging crookedly around her knees she suddenly seemed again the little girl I had always known and I almost shouted after her to come back. I stood and watched her; finally I went inside.

For several days I felt more awkward than ever walking with Aileen, the secret between us at once so dark and alluring that something inside me wanted to ask her for the prurient details, but also so burdensome that the knowledge of it almost filled me with guilt as if I myself had done the deed and needed to confess it. I looked at her walking beside me and wondered what she was thinking, but the only impression her face gave me was one of utter plainness. I knew that I had to do something; the thing was too heinous to be kept secret. But whom to tell? Certainly not my parents. It would have to be to a stranger. But whom?

Two days later I knocked on Mr. Charbonneau's door, unable to carry the weight inside any longer.

"Eddie! Come on in." He stepped aside to let me through. "Have a seat." He looked at me a moment as if waiting for me to begin, then he said, "Something on your mind?" He sat on the edge of his desk beside a large green blotter.

I had not wanted to jump into the matter so quickly, had hoped we could have chatted a while before I gradually steered the conversation to the topic. "Well, yeah," I said. "Somebody I know is—sort of in a spot."

"Hmm," he said. Then he waited again for me to speak. "You want to tell me about it?"

I wiped the palms of my hands hard on my pants. "I don't know just—well, maybe I should just—tell you. Her father—he makes her sleep with him." It was out, and hadn't been that difficult after all.

Mr. Charbonneau looked at me a moment, then got up off the desk. He moved to his chair, rested his elbows on the desk, and stared at me with his hands covering his mouth. He did not say anything and the buzz of the fluorescent lights was suddenly loud.

Then he said, "You want to tell me who it is?"

"Actually, I'd rather not." Aileen's father seemed perfectly capable of carrying out his threat.

Mr. Charbonneau gritted his teeth. "Tell me," he said, "is it Aileen Greve?"

I stared hard at him before being able to say anything. "How did you know?"

"I was afraid it was her," Mr. Charbonneau said with resignation. "But at the same time I'm relieved."

"I don't—what do you mean?"

"Eddie, I have to tell you something. You live right by Aileen, right?"

"Yes."

"Then you know what her home's like. Not good. Mother run away, father on welfare, sometimes beats his children, right? This will come as a surprise to you, but what Aileen said is not true."

"It isn't?"

"Right. It's not true. She told a teacher the same thing and we checked it out with a medical examination. It's not true. She made it up."

It took a few moments for what he said to sink in. Made it up? People made up such things? "Why would she do that?"

"It's hard to say. Could be a number of reasons. Maybe it's her way of making herself—well, we don't know." He stood up. "But I appreciate you coming to talk to me about it. You did the right thing. But in the meantime, it might be best if you tried to act as if nothing happened. Think you can do that?"

I was too confused to say anything as I walked out of his office.

The rest of that school year I walked with Aileen, side-stepping the potholes in our road. I'm not sure if she ever knew that I knew it was all a lie, and it has taken me a long time to realize how great her need must have been for her to do it. Even now I can still only guess at her reasons, but the lie doesn't seem all that terrible to me now, just very understandable, in its own illogical way.

I mentioned earlier that except for one time I never went into Aileen's shack, partly because my presence there would be an embarrassment to her and partly because I was afraid of what I would see. As I think back about it now, I realize suddenly that not once did Aileen ever step into our house either, kept so spotless by my mother, and I wonder whether it was because she felt that her presence was equally an embarrassment to me, but for the opposite reason. Maybe she too had been afraid of what she would see. After all, there is only one thing more frightening than chaos, and that is holiness.

THE WHITE RABBIT

The boy knew that his father must have looked funny to the young married men working at the factory. Every day after finishing his paper route the boy would stop his bike at the plant and wait for his father. At 5:30 the whistle on the roof blew with a shrill blast of steam, and a split second later the young men burst from the building, full of banter, combing their hair and lighting cigarettes, silver lunch pails squeezed between elbow and waist. Then they drove off in shiny cars.

Ten minutes later the boy's father appeared, alone, wearing his black beret and a grey striped suit too baggy for church but still too useful during the week to be thrown away. Then he mounted his black Dutch bicycle with the black plastic mud flaps encasing the chain and the top half of the rear wheel, and he pedalled the four miles home with the boy.

"How was it today?" the boy's grandfather asked when they got home.

"The same," his father replied. "All we did today was print milk cartons, ten hours of it. Tomorrow we do frozen fish cartons."

"Here you are, the best butcher in the country, and all you do is print little paper boxes," his grandfather snorted. "High time it is you left that place, Jaap."

"Ja, I know, but we can't yet."

The boy sensed his grandfather's impatience. Each day that dragged by without bringing to reality Opa's dream of a butcher shop in Canada only increased his misery, and he would sidle aimlessly through the house, muttering pronouncements at anyone or anything he thought needed them:

"Nieko, tie your shoelace! Next thing you know you will break your neck, and then see what kind of a medical bill we would have.

Unless the government pays for that too already!

"Joop, if you are going downstairs anyway, take an empty pail along and fill it with coal when you come back up. That's the trouble nowadays—nobody uses their heads anymore!"

He would sit in his living room chair, listening to records of psalms sung by a choir of Dutch fishermen. Or he would prop his high black shoes up on a hassock, his chin tilted sharply so that he could read through the bottom part of his bifocals. He spent hours reading the newspapers from Holland, but they only put him in a bad mood, for he saw little happening there of which he approved.

"Hhmmph!" he grunted. "Look at here. *Verdraait*, if the country isn't turning socialist. Those Nazis were one thing, but it's a good thing we left when we did, Jaap," he said to the boy's father. "Three civil servants for every decent working man. And for everything you need their permission. 'You want to build on your house an addition? Fill out an application. Paint your house yellow? Fill out a form. Remodel your bathroom? Come to our office.' Next thing you know we would need their permission to paint the toilet seat! And if they didn't like the colour of my piss after I eat beets, a *stommeling* of a civil servant we would have knocking on our door!"

"That's better than to do it by the tree in the back yard like you do now," the boy's mother said.

"Ach woman, what do you know about these things!" he flamed. "Stick to your cooking and your sewing and your silly perfumes!"

The boy noticed his father trying to keep Opa busy by giving him little jobs to do around the house, like painting a room or building a closet, but these chores were not his trade. His hands were clumsy with a brush or a hammer. A knife was another thing. A knife was almost part of his right hand, as if he had been born with one there.

One day the boy's father came home triumphantly with a white rabbit dangling from his outstretched hand. "Got it cheap from Reitsma," he said, and handed it to Opa. When the boy saw his grandfather head for the basement with the dead rabbit he knew something was about to happen. He followed stealthily and hid in the darkness at the top of the stairs.

He saw Opa string up the rabbit by the hind legs from a ceiling beam, then take two knives and sharpen them by honing them on each other rapidly, the blades flashing in miniature duel. Opa took one of the knives and made a slit through the fur at each heel, just below the noose, and along the hind legs. Then he stripped the white pelt off the rabbit just as a person strips off soiled garments, and the sound was like the ripping of cloth.

When Opa was done the boy was shocked by the nakedness of

the glossy red body dangling from the ceiling. Stripped of its coat it looked so small that the white fur still on its hind feet resembled baby bootees, but now grotesquely huge. The boy knew then that he could not eat of the rabbit.

His mother served it next day, with red wine to celebrate the event. She was surprised when he mumbled his no thanks.

"But Joop, it's good meat."

Opa did not let him off that easily. "Wait a minute, young man," he said in Dutch. "What do you mean you don't like it. Not good enough it is for you? Do you know what people would have given for this during the war? Men had their throats slit for less, do you know that?" and he rasped his thumb across his Adam's apple. His white hair bristled, his face was red with blood, and the loose flesh beneath his chin shook like the wattles of an old rooster.

At the end of the meal, as the boy's father was about to read the Bible passage, Opa took the Bible from his hand and turned to a different page. Then he looked around the table, and when he was satisfied that all were properly reverent he began to read, and the boy felt the cadence of the phrases as they seemed to rain down in blows upon his head: "O give thanks to the Lord for he is good . . . let the redeemed of the Lord say so . . . he gathered them out of lands . . . they wandered in the wilderness . . . and he delivered them . . . he led them by a straight way . . . let them thank the Lord . . . for he satisfies him who is thirsty, and the hungry he fills with good things."

Later in the evening when his father went to the basement the boy followed and asked why Opa was always so grouchy. "Things are a bit difficult for Opa right now," his father said, putting his arm around the boy's shoulder. "It's not easy for you to understand, I know, but Opa needs to have something to do, and maybe he felt insulted when you refused to eat the rabbit."

"I didn't mean it that way," the boy said. "Besides, he's grouchy all the time. And he's always talking about the War. Why does he have to talk about the War all the time?"

Then his father told him of what had happened to Opa during the War.

He needed to think about that, and he went upstairs. He lay on his bed and thought about what his father had just told him, about the bomb that had struck Opa's house during the War. It had come with a high whistle, and then smashed the house to burning rubble. After the explosion Opa regained consciousness and began to search frantically in the burning ruin for his wife and relatives. He found his wife buried to her shoulders under brick and rock. Minutes later she had died. Then the fire forced Opa out of the ruin, and he could only stand by helplessly. After the blaze had died down, townspeople went in to search for the victims. In one blow the boy's grandmother, three uncles, and three aunts had been killed.

He lay on his back, thinking, and he remembered suddenly the time he had played with wooden blocks on the living room floor when all at once he had heard the staccato beat of marching boots on the cobblestones outside, and when he ran to the window and pushed aside the white gauze curtains he saw the soldiers, the German soldiers in the street below, coming right toward him. He peered from just above the window sill, watching the soldiers march closer and closer until they were right below him in the street, the faces hard beneath the rakish helmets, the precise rows of rifles with bayonets pointing upwards, the boots pounding on the cobblestones, the thunderous clack clack clack ricocheting between the high brick buildings in the narrow street, then echoing in his ears like a snare drum, and he dropped beneath the window sill in fright and closed his eyes tight and clamped his hands over his ears, but still he heard the boots, as if he were in a bad dream with a train hurtling toward him without his being able to move, the train shrieking by at the last minute, the vibration pounding through his whole body, until the metal rhythm had receded. Finally he rose. The soldiers were gone.

He brooded over these things and felt again his fear of that time, so that he felt suddenly cold. And then he thought he began to understand a little bit better why Opa was the way he was. But with the understanding came revulsion, for his grandfather's world seemed at that moment to be made of blood.

His father's servitude to Laban, as Opa often put it, did not last seven years. After three years in the factory, his father was able to buy a store on the main street of the Fraser Valley town in which they lived.

On a raw day in late November they moved, hauling furniture and boxes out of the old house and moving them into the living quarters above the store. Even Opa carried whatever he could. The boy's mother kept telling him not to strain himself, to carry lighter objects, and please! to wear a scarf, but Opa shrugged her off: "*Ach, kind*, why don't you pack the kitchen things. We men will worry about the rest," he said, coughing as he helped guide the heavy pump organ onto the truck.

By mid-December the store was ready. Opa watched the painter put the finishing touches on the sign in the window: "Witte's Meats," the white letters painted in an arc just as they had been on the store window in Amsterdam.

The front of the store was brightly lit and often there was laughter, the boy's father presiding over the business with a ready wink in his eye. He would tell stories when the ladies of the congregation came in, for he was happy, and so were the women to have a Dutch butcher in town. They would hold a hand to their mouths as they laughed, self-consciously hiding the ill-coloured caramel gums of their dentures.

"Sausage just as you like it from the old country," the boy's father would say, "with not too much garlic in it!"

Opa, too, was a different man, and the boy sensed it as he watched him in back of the store. Opa did most of the actual butchering, taking the front and hind quarters that came from the packers and cutting them up into steaks, roasts, and chops.

The huge slabs of meat carried into the dusky cutting room both attracted and repelled the boy. He felt about the meat as he did about touching his tongue to a frozen bridge railing on the way to school: he knew the disastrous results of making contact, yet was inescapably drawn to do so. There was something both repulsive and magnetic about the huge carcasses hanging stiffly from the gleaming metal hooks in the cooler, red meat flecked with white fat, the purple liver, heart, and tongue dangling from the neck at the bottom. A pork chop lying under the front counter's stark fluorescent lights was one thing, but the meat carcasses hanging in the macabre light of the cooler resembled their former state closely enough to arouse fear in the boy. The smell of blood hung coldly in the air.

One day the boy stood in the cutting room watching Opa dress some meat, his frock so splotched with deep red blood it looked as if it had been washed in it. His accurate arm raised the cleaver and brought it down thwok! through a bone and onto the carving block. Then he went to the front of the store.

The boy approached the block, drawn to the slab of red meat. White lines of fat ran through it like a river on a map, thin streams radiating from the main one. He brought his forefinger to touch the meat, and was surprised by its softness and wetness. As he drew his hand away he saw the blood on his finger. He looked for a place to wipe it, not wanting to clean it on his pants, but there was no rag in the room. He turned his finger along the side of the carving block and left a thin, snaky line. He looked at the cleaver, tried to lift it by the handle, and found it unexpectedly heavy. He rasped his thumb lightly across the sharp edge, then quickly withdrew his hand when he felt the keenness of the blade on each thin line of his thumb-print.

Then Opa returned, adjusted the meat on the block, and began cutting off the fat, the thin knife slicing easily through the meat. His hands were covered with blood and moved deftly, without wasted motion. Then he took the meat to the front of the store, placed it in trays under the glass counter, and stepped into the cooler for another piece of meat.

He emerged cradling a slab of pork in his arms. When the huge door closed behind him with a clank the boy imagined what it would be like to be locked in the cooler; he saw himself pounding on the door, screaming to be freed from his dark and cold imprisonment with those hulking corpses.

Opa began sharpening his knives, just as he had done before skinning the rabbit, and the boy heard again the stripping of the pelt that was just like the sound of ripping cloth.

"Are you going to be a butcher when you grow up, Joop?" Opa asked him in Dutch.

He had not expected the question, and was unsure of just how much lay behind it. He was oldest son. How much had been decided for him?

"No, Opa," he said.

"Why not?"

"I don't know. Don't like it, I guess."

"What will you be then?"

He did not know what to say. He felt only a desire, still chaotic, for a cleaner world than that of his grandfather, a world of order and light and no blood.

He shrugged his shoulders.

"But you have to be **something**," Opa said.

Then the boy felt the blood rising to his cheeks, and he blurted, "Well, I'm not going to be a butcher, that's for sure! That's all you do—cut up dead animals!" and what he expected then was a cuff on the head, as if he had said something profane.

But he felt his grandfather's heavy hand, covered with dried blood, resting on his head, and he heard, "That's all right, *m'jongen*. There's no hurry. But for now, throw these pieces of fat into that pail over there, will you?"

The boy looked up at his grandfather from beneath the heavy hand. Opa seemed to mean it.

He gathered the pieces of fat into his hands, threw them into the pail, and ran upstairs. There he washed his hands.

The boy's bedroom was up in the third story of the house, and he was fond of looking out the window at the people on the sidewalk across the street far below. Especially that winter he felt warm and safe there high in his heaven.

He watched the white snow settle on the pavement. Smoke drifted from the chimneys across the street. He placed his cheek against the cold window and looked up to see the flakes, wondering where so many could possibly come from. When he looked down at the snow against the red brick storefronts the flakes were white and they drifted lazily down, but when he looked up into the sky they were dark and they swirled angrily about.

That particular Christmas they had much to celebrate, what with the opening of the store. The spruce tree stood high, its silver peak reaching the ceiling. They had decorated the tree all together, sprinkling tinsel through the branches and hanging ornaments and coloured balls, and when his mother lit the candles in the room, the glow reflecting in the many ornaments, it seemed to him the tree contained a thousand candles.

His mother baked almond ring and *gevulde koek* and iced mocha tarts, and when some friends from the congregation came for the day, the men smoking fat Dutch cigars and drinking red wine, the room hung heavy with a pall of cigar smoke, and the smell of wine filled the house as it does in church during Communion.

That evening he held his father's hand as they walked through the softly falling snow to church. His grandfather coughed again, and his mother said, "Opa, you should have worn your scarf," and he said to her, "Can't a man have a little cough nowadays?" In church, the many flickering candles made the boy drowsy so that he fell asleep, the soft notes of *Stille Nacht, Heilige Nacht* drifting into his ears as his head nodded and then fell against his father's arm.

Three days later the boy did not see his grandfather in the store. "Opa's not feeling well," his mother said, but he saw in her eyes the wild look of a small animal in fear.

That night he could not fall asleep. He left his door open and saw his mother hurrying in and out of Opa's room next to his with a hot water bottle or a glass of hot anise milk. Finally he fell into a fitful sleep.

In the middle of the night he awoke and heard a voice feebly singing, and it was some time before he recognized the voice as Opa's. His grandfather was singing Dutch psalms.

The boy lay there in the dark suddenly awake, transfixed by the scratchy voice singing slightly off-key. The voice pulled him out of bed; he tiptoed stealthily through the darkness to the next door. It stood ajar. He peeked into the room and saw his father with his back to him, standing by Opa's bed, and his mother sitting forward in a chair by the bed, holding Opa's hand. They did not see him, although he felt certain they would hear the pounding of the blood at his temples.

Opa lay propped against white pillows. He was dressed in a nightshirt white as the snow. His eyes were closed, and his head with its shock of white hair rolled slightly to and fro according to the rhythm of the thin melody escaping from his bloodless lips.

Then his grandfather began to sing the song of Simeon, familiar to the boy, for it had been sung in church that Christmas. After Opa finished the song in tremulous voice, the last frail notes seemed to hang frozen in the air.

The boy tiptoed back to his room. He climbed into bed and pulled the blankets over his head, for he felt he had seen a terrible beauty. And all he heard, over and over again, was the sound of the ripping of cloth.

FIRST SNOW

*"As the snow comes down from heaven . . . so shall
my word be."*
                                        Isaiah 55

To be perfectly honest, Dominee De Wolde did not at all like the
idea of having to spend his Monday driving thirty miles of back-
country Alberta roads just to find out what might have happened to
this fellow Tjepkema. Monday was his usual day off and he liked to
spend it in his study browsing leisurely through the church papers
from Holland or reading denominational journals like *Calvinist
Contact* and *De Wachter*, relishing the day's luxury of not yet
having to worry about next Sunday's sermons. But this morning he
would have to drive all the way out to Tjepkema's farm just to see
what had happened to the bachelor. To make matters worse, the
season's first snow had been predicted.

And so De Wolde was not in the best frame of mind as he ate his
breakfast. He asked his wife for a refill of coffee and tried to think of
some way he could avoid having to make the long drive. That
Tjepkema. "Just costs money," he had said about getting a telephone.

The problem was that Tjepkema had not been in church yesterday.
For most members of Dominee De Wolde's little congregation of
Dutch immigrants to miss the service would have been remarkable
enough, but for Tjepkema—well, everyone knew something had to
have happened. The man never missed.

When spring rains made the dirt roads impassable he bounced
into the church parking lot in his battered Chev pickup, its navy
blue body spattered with an inch-thick coat of black mud flaring
from the wheels. Even in blizzards, when others would be imprisoned

43

in their houses for days, Tjepkema showed up promptly at quarter to ten, appearing out of the swirling storm like a ghostly visitor from some strange planet, snow plastered to his hub caps, the load of firewood used for weight in the bed of his pickup flecked with white. Yes, something had to be wrong all right, for only the return of the Lord Himself would prevent Tjepkema from making it to church, and now De Wolde would have to find out what it was. Maybe the man had been eaten by one of his hogs.

They had delayed the service yesterday waiting for Tjepkema. His absence had been noticed at once for the congregation numbered only fourteen families. Dominee De Wolde had stepped into the narrow entry of the church, exchanging the usual words of greeting with his parishioners, and had felt their growing unease as the hour of ten approached with Tjepkema still absent. Then he retreated to the consistory room to don his black robe and to offer the customary prayer for the service with his two elders and two deacons, and when they had returned to the sanctuary the people had not taken their seats as usual but were standing silently at the rear of the church asking each other what might possibly have happened to Tjepkema.

Dominee De Wolde had prepared a sermon on I Corinthians 1 verse 21b: "It pleased God by the foolishness of preaching to save them that believe," and he was eager to give it, for he had worked hard on it. He approached the people at the back. "Shall we begin?" he said.

"Ja, Dominee," said Mr. Terpstra, "but where is Tjepkema?"

"I don't know. Shall we wait a few minutes yet?"

Half an hour later there was still no Tjepkema. People sang the opening psalms dispiritedly, stole concerned glances at each other during the reading of the Law, and seemed not at all comforted by the Assurance of Pardon. By the time Dominee De Wolde began his sermon he could tell that the people's hearts just weren't in listening, and therefore his wasn't in preaching, either. Afterwards, Mrs. Bouwsema had come up to him saying, "Mooie preek, Dominee, I never knew there was so much in that text—but where is Tjepkema?"

"Ja, Dominee, I enjoyed it too," said Mr. Langerak, "but what do you suppose happened to Tjepkema?"

Tjepkema, Tjepkema. Dominee De Wolde promised them he would look up Tjepkema tomorrow. And then he was angry at Tjepkema for spoiling his Sunday, for he had so looked forward to delivering his sermon. And now he would have to spend his Monday driving thirty miles of dirt road out to the man's farm and back again. With snow predicted.

De Wolde finished his coffee. He looked out the living room window to see what the weather was like. Eastward the sun rose in an arch of blue sky but in the west the horizon was steel grey. He'd better hurry. It was close to nine already, the children having left for school long ago.

He backed his car out of the driveway and drove slowly westward, his legs cold against the plastic seat cover. The town's few streets were made of hard-packed dirt and had no curbs, so that when he mowed his lawn in the summer and he came to the strip of grass close to the road the lawn mower made a loud clatter as it spat out a cloud of sand and rock. De Wolde looked at the houses on the street. They were small and white and it struck him suddenly that he hardly knew his neighbours. He saw them now and then weeding flower beds or raking leaves, and when he drove by he would nod at them politely, but he had never had a conversation with any of them and then he felt guilty, for he knew the Dutch had a reputation for being cliquish.

The lawns had all turned brown after weeks of frosty nights. De Wolde's car kicked up a few leaves as a sole reminder that there had ever been any and all he had to look forward to now was another long cold winter.

He drove through the town's business section, a single block of small stores, a Texaco gas station, a John Deere implement dealer, and the Bluebonnet Cafe, which would soon be filled with retired farmers who spent their winters sitting in the bare wooden booths smoking and complaining about grain prices. He wondered what enabled the people of the town to pass their whole lives in this small cluster of houses, stores, and grain elevators as minute on the prairie as an irritation on the skin of a giant.

At the edge of town he turned north on the highway. He would be able to follow it for only three miles before having to turn west onto dirt road again. Ahead, the sky had turned a deeper grey. He passed a drive-in movie on his left, its screen standing bleached and white against the sky. A sign on the theatre said "Closed For The Season" and as De Wolde looked through the open gate he caught a glimpse of rows of car microphones like a vast acre of parking meters, empty and desolate.

He had lived in this town six years now. Time soon to consider a call to another city, he felt, if one should come. This was his second congregation. The first had been in a town even smaller than this one, located in the central part of the province. It had not been the place he would have chosen just graduating from seminary, but it was the only church that had called him, the kind that could attract only young candidates, and he'd had no choice but to go.

After five years overtures from other churches had started to come but the first ones were from places situated no better than where he was, and he had declined them. When his present church asked him to come he had received no calls for two years, and by that time he was anxious to move.

To be honest, he did not feel at home here. He worked hard with the people and cared for them well, and it was not that he disliked them, but they were different. He had grown up in The Hague whereas these people had all come from farming communities in Friesland or Groningen or Overijssel. They had names like Fopma or Tuinstra or Elgersma and spoke English with a sharp Frisian accent, swallowing the ends of words. And they could be stubborn sometimes! Men like Tjepkema read the church papers even more closely than he did, arguing fine points of doctrine as impassionedly as the farmers in the Bluebonnet Cafe argued government farm policy. Good people they were, but without an ounce of subtlety.

Actually, his wife enjoyed it here, which surprised him, since she had grown up in Vancouver and he had always considered her a city person. When they had moved to his first congregation he had worried that she might not be able to adjust. Now, however, she lived small town life with vigour. Three times a week she drove out to a dairy farm just outside of town to pick up fresh milk in gallon jars, their lids sealed shut with wax paper. She baked bread with whole wheat flour, stone ground by a woman down the street. Nor was she too proud as minister's wife to visit The Economy Shop for second hand clothes for the children or to trade in their ice skates for larger ones whenever they outgrew them. And the children? This was the only life they had ever known. But for himself, every now and then he felt a pang of longing to be elsewhere and with different people.

He saw the turnoff ahead and slowed down. He had to wait for an approaching cattle truck and it passed him with a blast of air that rocked his car, bombarding him with swirling wisps of straw. Then he turned left, his tires picking up the sand of the frozen dirt road and sending a thousand needles against the underside of his car. Before him the road ran slightly downhill, dipped, then reappeared narrower in the distance, stretching as far as he could see. Twenty-seven miles yet.

Their church building wasn't much. It was a small wood-frame structure bought from the United Church three years before he had come. He would not have advised his congregation to buy it. In summer green flies buzzed against the windows and in winter the building was drafty and cold. Nor was Mrs. Koetje much of an organist, dear soul, playing on the Dutch pump organ which stood in a corner. But it would be unfair for him to ask his parishioners to build a new church with a pipe organ; most of them had mortgaged themselves to the teeth to buy their farms.

De Wolde had hoped for a call from a church in Edmonton—or better yet, Hamilton or Toronto, where he would receive a congregation made up of city people: store owners, accountants, businessmen. Those he understood. And while he was hoping, he wished for a larger congregation too, since his preaching style was not suited for a small audience.

That was one thing his zeal had not diminished for: preaching. He lived for it. He worked hard on his sermons, spending long hours poring over the Dutch commentaries that lined the walls of his study. And the larger the audience the more eloquent he became, not with mere oratory, but with a passion to reveal the depth of the Word. As his father had always done.

His father had been minister in a large *Gereformeerde Kerk* in The Hague. An imposing structure it was, always filled to capacity, for his father was a renowned preacher. De Wolde remembered how his father climbed the oak steps of his pulpit, careful not to step on the hem of his black robe, and when he spoke the familiar words of the opening invocation, *"Onze hulp is in de Naam des Heere,"* then raised his hands for the blessing, his wide velvet sleeves fell back from his arms. The organ pipes rose high behind the pulpit and De Wolde remembered that as a boy he used to wonder if air came out of the neat rectangular openings, for the pipes so resembled steam whistles. The church had a famous organist who played soaring preludes, and when the people sang psalms the music rolled through the high-ceilinged church. Then his father preached the sermon, beginning always with the salutation "Beloved congregation," the way he almost sang it in Dutch: *"Geliefde geMEEN - te"* and then the congregation sat silent for the next forty minutes, held by his voice. Even though De Wolde had not always understood what his father was saying, he knew already as a boy that he too wanted to become a preacher. But when the time had come for him to enter university to prepare for the ministry, his father's eminence appeared suddenly before him as an insurmountable obstacle, and he decided to emigrate to Canada. He would become the Dominee De Wolde of that country.

Dominee De Wolde. Even after fourteen years in the ministry he found the title strange, for he had always heard it used with such awe for his father. And now here he was, in Alberta, driving through the middle of empty prairie just to find out what might have happened to this fellow Tjepkema.

He saw something black at the edge of the road ahead. As he came closer he saw that it was a dog, and when he passed by, it charged out of the grass and ran alongside his car, yapping at the left front wheel. One of his elders, a farmer named Flikkema, had once told him how to cure a dog of doing that. "Wait until he slows down," Flikkema had said, "and just as he's by your door you open it quick and send him flying. He'll never chase a car again." But De Wolde could not bring himself to do it, and after a last frantic bark the dog gave up the chase.

Tjepkema. What could have happened to the man? A strange fellow he was with his blond hair lying in a thatch on top of his head, then cut in a sharp line high above his ears like a monk, as if he sheared it himself. He never looked dressed, not even in a suit, which only made him appear incongruously formal for the farmer that he obviously was. In church he always occupied a third row seat, and when the sermon began he would fold his arms and cross his legs and sit stone still in concentration, looking at De Wolde with intent eyes as if he might be the only one there.

Thirty-four and still a bachelor. How did the man expect to find a wife here in the middle of nowhere? In Edmonton, yes, even in Red Deer, where the churches were larger and he might meet a young woman. But stuck out here on his farm with his hogs? De Wolde had to hand it to him, though, driving those sixty miles every week, even on Wednesday evenings for Men's Society. And the way he spoke in the meetings—the man might be a pig farmer with a clipped Frisian accent, but he obviously read the theology books and even the books of sermons he borrowed regularly from De Wolde. A candidate for elder he would have been, in fact—had he been married.

But what could possibly have happened to him? Ach, it was probably nothing serious. Flu, maybe, or some other little thing that could happen to anybody. But De Wolde knew at once it would have to be more than that. Tjepkema was strong as an ox. Had to be, with the long days he put in. His farm showed it, too, even in the short time he'd owned it. The last time De Wolde had come out to see him with an elder for *huisbezoek* Tjepkema had proudly taken them around the place, pointing out the yard he had spruced up by hauling off broken machinery that had lain tangled in wild grass, and showing how he had cleaned out the barn and built new hog pens so that now he had not a bad operation going. Even De Wolde could see that.

He had driven a number of miles before he became aware suddenly that the sun had disappeared long ago and that the daylight had taken on a strange hard edge. The objects he saw out of his window — fence posts, the stones on the side of the road, the brown fields themselves — seemed at once colder and starker than when he had left town. The landscape looked as if the wind had blown it flat and had scoured it clean in preparation for some profound and violent change.

Then De Wolde knew something terrible had happened to Tjepkema. His tractor had rolled, pinning him underneath. He had been clearing the trees west of his place and the chain saw had jumped, burying itself in his leg, and he had dragged himself halfway back to the house before bleeding to death in the field. He'd been working in the loft of his barn — hadn't he said he wanted to put in a new floor there? — and he'd fallen, cracking his skull open on the cement floor thirty feet below. He'd been gored in the chest by a bull. Maybe he did get eaten by one of his hogs. De Wolde had seen some of these farm accidents in his fourteen years in Alberta, and nothing would surprise him. Ask the widows he'd had to comfort after their husbands had died the most freakish and violent deaths.

De Wolde bent forward to look up out of the windshield, as if to make sure that God was still in heaven after he had entertained such gruesome thoughts, but all he saw overhead was cold grey sky. He glanced back and saw the same and then he felt utterly alone, as if God had indeed fled, forsaking him in this vast, empty prairie. Instinctively he pressed harder on the gas pedal; he looked at his odometer and noted with relief that he had only three miles to go.

He drove as fast as the dirt road would permit, keeping his eye open for Tjepkema's place. It did not come, and it did not come, until he began to wonder whether he had passed it, knowing he could not have — and then he saw it in the distance, the outline of the grey barn and the small house in front of it standing cold and stark against the eerie mid-morning darkness. As soon as he saw the house he drove more slowly, scanning the yard and field in hope of seeing Tjepkema normally at work, but he saw no one. When he entered the yard by the twin posts guarding the driveway he was almost afraid to go further, and he slowed his car to a grave ministerial crawl, like a hearse entering a cemetery. The yard lay hushed as if in Sunday calm.

He stopped his car by the house, wondering where he should look for Tjepkema first. In the barn, probably.

He was just about to slide out of his car when he saw the last thing he had expected. The front door of the house opened, and there stood Tjepkema. Dressed in his grey Sunday suit.

De Wolde was nonplussed. What did the man think he was doing dressed in his suit on a Monday morning?

"Dominee!" Tjepkema yelled from the porch. "Come on in!"

De Wolde stepped from his car and climbed the porch's wooden steps slowly, as if he might be ascending a pulpit, then stepped into the house. Tjepkema closed the door behind them. De Wolde smelled chopped wood. And hogs.

"Have a seat," Tjepkema said, pointing to the kitchen table. It was covered with a creamy white plastic tablecloth marked by coffee cup rings. De Wolde sat down, his elbows off the table.

"Coffee?" Tjepkema asked from the counter, running water into the sink.

"Please," De Wolde said. After his drive he was ready for a cup. Tjepkema took a piece of wood from the pile beside the stove, lifted the lid by the iron handle, and inserted the wood. Then he placed the kettle on the stove. "Hope you don't mind instant," he said.

"No no, that's fine."

Tjepkema removed two cups and saucers from deep in a cupboard above the sink, then examined the cups and blew into them. "Sugar?" he said.

"Yes, please." De Wolde looked around him. The kitchen was dark, but warm. Against the wall hung a calendar adorned with a picture of Lake Louise. The days of the month had been crossed off so neatly in pen it looked as if Tjepkema had decided to do them all at once.

De Wolde had not heard the water boil on the stove before Tjepkema took the kettle and poured. The coffee did not steam when placed on the table.

"Sorry I have nothing *lekkers* to go with the coffee," Tjepkema said. "I usually don't have any."

"That's all right," De Wolde said, tasting the lukewarm liquid. "This is fine. Besides, that's what I get for coming unannounced." He thought Tjepkema might take the hint and explain his absence, but the bachelor sat down on the opposite side of the table and said nothing, seemingly content to drink his coffee. De Wolde saw he wore a red tie with a picture of a snow-capped mountain painted on it.

"Zo," Tjepkema said after several sips, "town's still the same?"

"Still the same," De Wolde said.

Then neither of them spoke, as if waiting for the other to declare his intentions. Finally De Wolde could stand it no longer. "Listen," he blurted, "people wondered where you were yesterday."

Tjepkema looked suddenly uncomfortable, as if he had been caught in a private act. "Ja, Dominee, I was going to tell you about that," he said. He waited again, as though the matter he was about to tell were so serious he had to choose his words carefully. "What happened yesterday," he said, "was that I thought it was still only Saturday, and I worked all day in the barn. Then after I did my chores this morning thinking it was Sunday and I turned on the radio to listen to "The Back to God Hour" like I always do while I get shaved and dressed for church, here was the radio announcer telling me it was Monday! What a country it is, eh Dominee, with these distances."

He paused, as if overwhelmed by the enormity of his sin, then he continued. "So there was only one thing to do. I would have to let today be my Sunday. As a matter of fact, I just put on my suit to read a sermon when you drove in. And now that you're here, **you** might as well read it. I always get so much more out of it when I hear you."

"Well . . ."

"No, come now," Tjepkema said, his mind obviously made up. He walked into the living room, and then De Wolde had no choice but to follow.

"I chose a sermon by Dominee Van Harten of Hamilton," Tjepkema said. He handed De Wolde the booklet containing the sermon. "Go ahead now and read," he said, "I'll just sit here and listen." He folded his arms and crossed his legs and looked at De Wolde with intent eyes.

De Wolde sat down, casting a glance of discomfort at the window.

It was then he saw the first snow. He had forgotten all about it.

It came in hardly noticeable wisps at first, as if the weather had made a mistake and would hastily apologize before returning to normal. De Wolde looked at the sermon booklet, then at Tjepkema, and saw that the man was oblivious of the weather, waiting for him to begin. He would have to read.

"Beloved congregation," he began, uncertain whether he should have omitted the salutation. He felt naked without his robe. "Our text is taken from Hebrews 4 verse 12: '*For the word of God is living and active, sharper than any two-edged sword . . . discerning the thoughts and intentions of the heart.*'"

He looked again out of the window and saw that after the first phantom flecks of snow, the wind, keen as the edge of a knife was now hurling large flakes that seemed to bombard the house, hard and white and cruel.

He turned to the sermon and resumed reading.

CRACKED WHEAT

. . . and He to end all strife
The purest wheat in Heaven, His dear-dear Son
Grinds, and kneads up into this bread of life.

—Edward Taylor

My first day in Victoria is one of the hottest of the summer. Heat rises from the pavement in sheets so that cars glide toward me in a blur, floating ghostlike above the shimmering street. My tires swish in the melted tar, then pick up pea gravel and throw it against the underside of the van with a clatter. Even away from the city centre there is virtually no breeze. And all of the day's heat seems to find its way into my van, especially the black vinyl seat which scorches me every time I sit down after a call. The back of my shirt is wet and clings to the seat. Three o'clock, I tell myself. By three o'clock a cold can of pop.

That morning early I caught the first ferry out of Tsawassen to spend a week, my last of the summer, doing Fred Malkoske's bread route. Despite the heat my day goes well, mainly because Fred has given me accurate directions. Most drivers on vacation keep their books up to date, but every now and then the directions are so botched they might just as well not be there at all.

I'm not sure just how long it takes Fred to do the route, but judging from the pile of pages done I feel I'm making good time. That's a bit of a thing with me. Each day I try to finish earlier than the last. That means hustle. Open the back door of the van with the right hand, swing in the metal basket full of bread and pastry with the left, close the door, all in a smooth motion, then run to the front and write down the sale in the book. One thing about relief driving, too, is that you never get to know the customers well enough that you're forced to spend hours talking to them. One or two weeks and you're gone to another route.

I flip the page after a call and read the directions: "Go 2 mi. TR into naval base, 3d on L." I look at the odometer, mentally add two miles, and after passing a road sign that says "Entering Esquimalt" I find the road one tenth of a mile beyond the two. Good old Freddie.

As soon as I make the turn I know I'm right because all the houses are exactly the same. Not a middle class suburb kind of same, but a more military uniformity, coldly efficient and impersonal, each house with grey stucco at the top and dull blue siding at the bottom.

The women come to the door with baby clutched to hip or with hair curled high around frozen orange juice tins or with portable TV blaring dumb soap operas from the kitchen counter, all of the women numbly taking their white sliced, which is horrible gluey stuff, then retreating into the anonymity of their identical houses.

One breaks the pattern. The route book says the name is Mrs. Borelli and that she takes cracked wheat, one of the few I sell. I walk up the steps off the driveway and knock on the screen door, thinking that anybody who eats cracked wheat can't be all bad.

A woman opens and says, "Oh yes, let me get the money."

I watch her through the screen door but my eyes are used to the bright sunlight so that the kitchen is nothing but a green haze and I can't quite make her out as she rummages through her purse. I see only a pair of white, sharply creased slacks. They come to the door.

"Can you change a five?" the woman asks.

I open the screen door, wedge the basket between my hip and the doorpost, and reach into my pocket for the change.

"I'll tell you what," Mrs. Borelli says, "why don't you step in out of the sun. That way the flies don't come in either." I do as she says and she looks at me. "My, but you look hot. And no wonder. It's supposed to get up to 94 today."

"Yeah, it's pretty mean out there. Feels nice and cool in here, though." My neck feels chafed where the sweat drips into the irritation caused by my shaving.

"Would you like a cold drink?" she asks.

"I'd love one, if it isn't too much trouble."

"Not at all. Why don't you sit down a moment." She doesn't ask me, but says it, as if there's no question.

She clunks two ice cubes into a glass, pours in some Coke, and hands it to me, the pop fizzing in the ice. Then she sits down on a red stool by the counter, feet resting on one of the rungs, shoulders hunched forward like a little bird. She lights a cigarette and I watch her. Her hair is red, hanging loose to her shoulders, the sides swept forward, nicely, to two points. The fingers holding the cigarette by her chin are long and thin; her other hand lies palm up on her knee, the blue veins at her wrist standing out like cords pulled taut between her elbow and hand.

"Are you a relief driver with the bakery?" she asks.

"Yeah, I do this during the summers. I'm a student."

Usually people are impressed by this answer and are content to leave it at that. But she asks me whether I go to UVic here.

No, I tell her, I live in Vancouver, which is an honest answer, but also an evasive one, I know.

She persists. "You go where then, UBC?"

At that point I realize I'll have to explain. I tell her that I attend a church-related college in the States and that I'm in a pre-seminary program.

I'm not sure what she'll say to that, if her reaction to religion is as squeamish as most people's. But she startles me completely by saying, "Well, delivery man or minister, either way you give people bread, right?"

Now, I've not thought of that before. As a matter of fact, the last two summers I've begun to feel almost as if I were living in two worlds which hardly seem to touch each other: nine months I live as a student in a world abstract, systematic, and therefore governable; my summers delivering bread, however, are concrete and often chaotic, a mere means to an end, which violates the teaching of my upbringing that **all** of life is holy vocation. And therefore, once I see beyond the ingenuity of her metaphor, I realize that it contains a deeper truth that instantly bridges my two seemingly alien worlds.

The shock of recognition of the meaning of her words must have shown in my face, for Mrs. Borelli says with a trace of amused complicity, "We're Catholic. Not very good ones, but still Catholic."

But I'm feeling only the shame of realizing that my practice has been inconsistent with my belief, and I guess the rest of what I'm recounting here demonstrates how difficult it is to evict the contradictions that lodge stubbornly as squatters in our lives.

The bakery route is divided into two runs, a M-W-F one and a T-Th. The next day all goes well on the T-Th run. It's the shorter of the two and I finish at five o'clock.

Wednesday morning I load beside Kenny Greene. "How's it goin'?" he says.

"Not bad. No problem so far."

The sky is clear and a cool morning breeze blows in off the harbour. Later it will be hot again.

"You managin' to get rid of the load O.K.?"

"I had a bit left over yesterday, probably because of the heat. Too many people at the beach. But I'll get rid of it at a freezer call today, so no sweat."

"Just make sure so's none a the customers runs their bill yea high. I been at this goin' on twenty years, and you gotta watch summa them. They'll skip out on ya and leave ya holdin' a bill for fifteen lousy bucks."

"Yeah, I'm watching it pretty well." What does he think I am, a rookie?

Then Kenny looks at me out of the corners of his eyes. "You got a girl back home? Must be tough durin' the week, huh?" and he laughs.

"I don't have a girlfriend, actually."

"Aw c'mon, a young fella like you? Don't gimme any a that. Besides, who needs a girlfriend? I know what's happenin' at the universities these days. I wasn't born yesterday ya know."

I laugh, letting Kenny interpret it any way he wants.

The day turns out to be another scorcher, the van so hot that it feels as if it should be baking the bread, not just carrying it. But I make good time and am ahead of schedule when I reach Mrs. Borelli.

"The usual," she says to me from inside. I wait on the steps, then she opens the screen door, takes the bread, and gives me the exact change.

"You look like you could use a repeat on that cold drink," she says, and stands aside holding the screen door open so that I can carry my basket through.

I hesitate. I seldom oblige when people invite me in because I hate to finish late. But I know her kitchen is cool and a cold drink sounds good, so I step inside, placing my basket gently on the red-tile floor so as not to scratch the wax finish.

She pulls back a chair for me, goes to the refrigerator, and takes a glass out of the top freezer. Then she pours in the drink. When she brings the glass to me it's covered with a glaze of frost, and I'm moved by her thoughtfulness. She had it all ready for me.

"How did you know to take cracked wheat to the door the first day?" she asks.

Her hospitality and warmth have made me feel loose and I tell her, "The moment I saw your house I said to myself, this looks like a cracked wheat kind of place," but as soon as I say it I remember the similarity of the houses in the base, and I'm not sure whether that makes my attempt at a joke even funnier or totally absurd. With panic I think the latter.

But she laughs. She sits down on the stool, her red hair swept back this time over her ears and gathered at the back as if she might be an artist. Her face is deeply tanned and she looks cool.

"You must be almost done for the summer, I guess."

"That's right. Matter of fact, this is my last week. Monday I head back to school."

"And here you haven't even told me your name," she says, feigning offense.

"Oh yeah. Sorry. Neil. Neil Van Wyk."

"Van Wyk—is that Dutch?"

"Uh huh. My parents immigrated in '52."

"That means that you were born there, too, right?"

"Yeah, I was five when we immigrated."

She drops her chin then and smiles, as if to tease me, and says, "Supposed to be hard-working people, the Dutch."

"No more than anybody else, I imagine. But they do have a mania about keeping things clean. You should see my mother. She even scrubs the driveway."

We both laugh. I'm surprised to find myself conversing with this woman as an equal. In high school the girls had always seemed so sure of themselves, so carefree, while I had been reticent, aware of being Dutch and therefore different, so I thought. But with this woman I'm feeling at ease.

"How about you—you must be Italian, with a name like Borelli."

"I'm not, but my husband is."

Then it's my turn to tease. "I didn't think Italians had red hair."

"But with a woman you never know, do you," she says point blank, and immediately I feel her superiority as a woman and I don't know just what to say then. I look around self-consciously. Children's art work covers one of the glossy red walls. There is a paper mosaic of a sailor in white bell-bottoms, the hands large where the child had difficulty cutting the pieces small enough. Beneath the sailor the word "daddy" is printed in a child's scrawl. Beside it, a sheet of red paper shows Humpty-Dumpty sitting on a brick wall, the oval shape made of little pieces of eggshell glued to the paper.

"Your kids'?"

"Yes. Hanging things up encourages them. The egg thing was done by Danny, who's eight, and the others are Gina's. She's ten. They did them at the park. There's a really fine summer arts and crafts program there, and the kids just love it. What with it and the swimming pool, they spend all afternoon there, and I mean all afternoon. I don't know whether to enjoy the peace and quiet, or hate the loneliness."

She lights a cigarette, blows out the smoke slowly through pursed lips, and seems suddenly pensive, as if she's all by herself. Then she says, still not looking at me, "Have you ever wished you could be a little child again? Seriously—just be able to do your life over again?"

I'm not sure I have ever felt that.

"I sometimes wish I could," she says. Her eyes turn away from me and narrow, as if they're bad and she's trying to focus on an object far in the distance. "But then again, maybe things wouldn't be all that different. Because you wouldn't know then what you do now, would you."

I tell her I suppose not.

"It sure would be nice, though," she muses.

"What would you do different?" I ask her. It's hard for me to imagine my own life being much different from what it has been, as if past events had an unquestioned inevitability.

"Well, I would study, like you. I had always intended to—Well, I wouldn't have gotten married so soon, for another."

"Would you really?"

"Yes, I was crazy!" Her voice turns husky in self-reproof. "Romantic fool that I was, falling in love with a sailor's uniform. And me only nineteen."

Only nineteen. I wonder how old she thinks I am.

"I look at the children now," she says, "and I remember what it was like, how we trusted everything and everyone. It was easier to believe, somehow, back then. In yourself, other people—do you know what I mean? You just didn't doubt that things could be any different from the way they were—or should be. Everything fit. Same with the church. Somehow, when the priest spoke, you were certain, and when you felt the host on your tongue—oh, I had visions of the broken body!"

Her eyes stare wide at nothing in particular and her impassioned tone surprises me, embarrasses me. I don't know just what to say to her, feel totally incapable of forming any words even though I want to, and to leave seems at that moment such a temptation all of a sudden.

"Listen, I **have** to run. I've got a few hours to go yet, and it's way past three." It's an awkward time to leave, and my clumsiness shows it.

But her embarrassment is equal to mine, as if she were caught in a secret. "I'm sorry," she says, "I didn't mean to detain you."

"That's all right. I forgot about the time. I'll see you Friday."

I step out, carefully closing the screen door so the spring will not make it slam.

I finish the route half an hour later than before.

"They didn't send me my two lousy pumpernickel," Kenny Greene complains to me Friday morning as we load our trucks. "They never give me what I order. So what am I supposed to tell the customer? Huh? You tell me."

"Yeah, bad news."

"Bloody right. Hey, I almost forgot! Last day on the Island right? So, poor Freddie's coming back to the grind Monday. Well, every party's got to end sometime. Right?"

"I suppose."

I continue loading my van. White sliced on the left, where I can reach them easily; beside them the brown sliced, then the assorted: whole wheat, sesame seed, buttertop, and unsliced fancy.

I want to get an early start. My last day. Of all days to catch the early ferry home this is the one. But I'd have to make good time— and not have too many tourists at the ferry slip in Swartz Bay.

Kenny breaks my daydream. "Weekend comin' up, eh? Some fast action, I bet!"

I try to ignore him.

"Hey, the Mainland girls any better than the Island ones you saw? Huh? You shouldn't leave so quick. You're not gettin' a taste of the local talent." Then he comes close to me, nudging me in the ribs with his elbow. "Well, it's probably just as well you're leavin' cuz all those lonely babes in the naval base'll be havin' the hots for ya purty soon. Yeah, whaddya expect with all the hubbies havin' a good time over there in the Mediterranean and them places. You think the ladies ain't missin' it? Huh? You didn't know that, didja. Smart university kid!"

I finish loading and swing shut the doors of my van. "See ya, Kenny. Take care."

"Yeah, be good. Hey, and take it easy on the ladies!"

The route goes smoothly. The weather is hot but not uncomfortable. I arrive at Mrs. Borelli's house an hour earlier than usual and she's surprised to see me.

"Oh, you've caught me early," she says. "I must look a fright!" She runs a comb through her hair and brushes her slacks nervously with her hand. Then she says for me to sit.

I feel on edge. My intentions are not to stay—at least, not for long, because I'm on the verge of having completed my summer job, and if I can only finish it now, the little left, I'll be free. But I also know that I've enjoyed talking with her and that she intends for me to stay and that she'll be disappointed if I don't.

"Well, your last day," she says, placing the cold drink on the table in front of me. "It's a special occasion, and I've got a little something for you. I was going to wrap it but you came too early." She seems awful fidgety, then walks to the counter and says, "Close your eyes now, and don't open them until I say."

I close my eyes. I hadn't expected this, whatever it is.

"This is for you," she says, holding out a book. Hardbound. Maritain. "I hope you like it."

I riffle through the pages, shaking my head.

"I know, I shouldn't have done it, right? But I wanted you to have it." She sits down on the stool, not at the counter this time but with me at the table. I smell her perfume, aware of it for the first time. "I—that's very good of you."

She does not say anything, content for the moment to watch me and enjoy my surprise at her gift. But I'm thinking desperately of something to say, anything just so I can break the silence.

"Well, Monday I travel."

She does not speak and again I feel the burden to talk.

"I guess your husband travels a lot."

"Yes, he does," she says, forcing a smile.

"Where's he stationed now?"

"Cyprus."

I feel awkward about the conversation, such as it is, but it seems to be steering itself and all I can do is plunge on.

"When will he be home?"

"October."

"Phew!"

"Yes, I know."

"What do you do, have a part-time job? I mean, how do you manage to fill the time?"

Her lip curls in a rueful smile. "In a way, filling the time is not really . . . Well, you learn to do a lot on your own. And don't forget there's the kids. They permit you to do only so much. But otherwise? I read a fair bit, make some of my own clothes . . . It's funny, though, it's not until you're by yourself that you discover how many social things assume you come in twos. And if you don't, you don't fit. Even at the parish. What I get there is sympathy, and that I don't need. You can't break loneliness with sympathy. You can't invite it over for a cup of coffee."

At that moment I sense how different her life is from mine and how hard it is for me to meet hers. Besides, what can I do in my last visit, such a brief moment. Behind her on the wall the second hand of the clock glides in a smooth, inexorable arc, and to go seems so inviting, to glide as smooth as the second hand, and I rise slowly.

"It's getting on and I want to thank you very much," I tell her, but she places her hand lightly on my arm, urging me back to my seat.

"Are you always this way?" she asks.

"What, you mean—?"

"Rushing off. Relax! Time goes fast enough without you pushing it."

I tell her no really, I should go, and that I'm grateful—and then her expression softens and she looks suddenly fragile and thin. Then she rises slowly from her stool, head down, comes close to me and places her hands on my elbows, and when she raises her head to look at me I'm surprised to see that her eyes are wet and staring into mine with a desperation I have never seen before. Then she draws me to herself and her hands are on my back and I hold her, close my eyes and smooth her hair with my hand, her lips on my neck—and suddenly I see Kenny Greene's leering face and remember his words and I jerk back my arms in shock.

Mrs. Borelli slumps down on the stool, weeping, hair over her face, and I feel I can't leave like this, not without her letting me go and saying that it's all right, and I walk to her stool and touch her shoulder. She doesn't move, and then I'm torn about what to do.

I run out. The screen door snaps shut behind me, and when I hear the clap I wince, as if the broken hand of Christ himself had slapped me in the face.

HOMESICKNESS

It **is** true that my father wasn't the usual Dutch-Canadian immigrant. "Hey Hennie," he said to me one evening after supper, "want to go down and help me mount a bird I shot? A red-tailed hawk, you should see it."

My mother was not feeling well again and sat by the living room window in her stiff-bristled, maroon velour chair. Supper dishes were still on the table and I knew she would not be of a mind to get at them.

"I'd better do the dishes first," I told him, fiercely proud he had asked me, a girl, and not my older brothers.

"Leave them," he said, "I'll help you with them later," and I followed him downstairs.

He was an outdoorsman and spent days in the bush. Hunting deer with a rifle had become too easy, had lost its challenge for him so now he used a bow, a beautifully laminated recurve bow. I loved to run my fingers over its glass-like smoothness, the tips curved like miniature skis. The arrows were black with splotches of green for camouflage, and he pointed out to me how the feathers didn't run straight along the shaft but curved slightly so the arrow would rotate and fly true through the air. The tips were shaped like the head of a harpoon, the barbs sharp as razor blades. During hunting season he would leave for the bush wearing a buckskin coat and a leather glove with the first three fingers cut off so he could pull the bowstring. I longed to go with him. I asked him how he hunted deer and he explained how he scouted them until he knew exactly where they bedded, where they fed, in what directions they moved, explained how he took a stand in a tree and when a deer got within range he would aim for the chest cavity and if he got in a good shot he tracked the blood spoor until he found the deer, dead from hemorrhage.

63

He would not take any of us hunting with him, and although I knew
it was because I was too young I was not content, already jealous of
the day my brothers might but I would not.

On the wall of his den he had hung animals, all of which he'd
mounted himself. "The trick is to give them **expression**, Hennie," he
would tell me. "Anyone can stuff an animal, but it takes an **artist** to
give them expression. Take those ptarmigan now, see how the one
looks startled?" Two of them stood on a piece of wood, one pecking
at the ground, the other indeed looking up as if frightened. "And
that owl, what would you say he is?" A great horned owl stared
down at me with black eyes peering from beneath beetled brows,
two tufts of feathers on top of its head like cowlicks of hair that
would not sit down. *Haughty* was the only word that came to me
and when I told my father, hoping it was right, he seemed pleased.
After that, the other animals were easy. On a branch sat a Swainson's
hawk, beak curved and sharp as if carved by knife, its head cocked
to one side in curiosity. On another wall hung a bobcat, teeth bared
in a snarl, beside it a wolf with similar expression, ears pulled back
in ferocity.

My father picked up the red-tailed hawk, its head lolling, and
placed it on its back. He separated the feathers on its breast just as I
might part my hair, then he took a razor blade and cut the skin from
the hawk's throat to its vent, and for the next hour I stood beside
him watching his hands meticulously free the skin from the body
until it was totally loose except for at the neck, where it hung like a
cape. Then came the part I found difficult to watch. He took his wire
nippers, curved the blades around the hawk's neck, and squeezed
hard with a *clip!*, cutting through the neck. He placed the headless
body, glistening and pink and shockingly small, in a pail. Then with
a piece of coat hanger he poked around inside the hawk's skull to
remove the brain, the scratching sound raising goose pimples on my
arms. The brain fell out like a ball of snot. Finally he popped out the
hawk's eyes with a scalpel.

"Get me the excelsior, will you," he said, and I went to the
cardboard box full of wood shavings used to wrap our dishes when
we came over from Holland. He would use the excelsior to fashion
the hawk's new body. He began treating the bird with Borax,
rubbing the powder into its skin and skull, while I looked for a pair
of hawk eyes: on the workbench were a number of small plastic
cases, like the ones fishhooks are kept in, labelled with animals'
names and containing my father's collection of artificial eyes. I
loved to look at them as if they might be precious stones, deer eyes
murky brown fringed with black, an almost fluorescent blue line

running through the pupil; pheasant eyes, the yellow iris speckled
with darker orange; and wood duck, black pupil in the centre of a
crimson iris. My favourite one was the coyote's eyes, which had a
yellow iris freckled with tiny brown spots like egg yolk sprinkled
with paprika, and a black pupil with a bright blue dot in the centre.
In one box I found a pair of hawk eyes, shiny and pure, which my
father would insert in the skull once he'd filled it with clay.

He would finish the hawk another time, and began to clean up. I
walked to the geological survey maps he had cut and pasted to fit
precisely together on a wall, forming a squiggly pattern of brown
lines running over swirls of green, white and blue. He had shown me
exactly where on the map our place was and when I looked at it I felt
proud, as if the government had given our home official recognition.

We lived on four acres on a gravel logging road in the Fraser
Valley miles north of the farms along the river, all around us
coniferous forest. My father worked in a small sawmill. Twenty
yards from our house stood a barn in which we kept a sorrel mare
named Brandy which I rode around the pasture, and two milk cows
named Wilhelmina and Flo. My father milked the cows every
morning but afternoon milking was my brothers' chore. After the
school bus dropped us off at the highway and we walked the gravel
road to our place I changed into an old shirt and pair of pants, put
on my black rubber boots, and waded through the snow in my
brothers' footsteps to the barn where they would bury their faces
into the cows' flanks as the first milk hit *psing! psing!* against the
bottom of the pail. The barn was an old thing with dirt floors and
cobwebbed walls. Perhaps because we had all witnessed the elemental
processes of mating and birth here, the barn seemed the natural
place for us to declare our secret feelings, some more openly than
others, my oldest brother Leonard scribbling his message inside the
door in white chalk: L.V. + A.S. while a contradictory warning was
posted by Billy and Karl:

PRIVATE GIRLS
KEEP OUT

Upstairs in the hayloft I told my friend Audrey Osinga my secret
loves.

Beside the barn stood a whitewashed shed in which my father
kept chickens, a dozen or so white Babcocks that provided our eggs.
The animal we enjoyed most, however, was a young black and

white goat we kept tethered in the front yard during the summer to nibble grass. He would jump onto our backs if we hunched down on all fours and had a habit of snuffling in our pockets to steal goodies, so we called him Dief, the Dutch word for "thief." The name was doubly appropriate, however, for even as a kid the goat resembled an old man with buck teeth, reminding us of Prime Minister Diefenbaker.

"Oh that's terrible," my mother said when she heard of it. She thought it disrespectful to make fun of the government and still had a picture of the Dutch royal family on the buffet in the living room.

The outside of our house was covered with unpainted shingles weathered to a dark brown, and whenever my father had to replace one the new shingle stood out like a piece of skin that had not suntanned normally along with the rest. Against the north wall of the house, the front, my father stacked a pile of wood every fall, providing our winter fuel. One Christmas we had such a snowfall my father had to shovel it off the roof, and he proudly held up a shovelful while my mother took his picture. When he was done he did not need to climb back down the ladder but just jumped off the roof into the snow, burying himself up to his waist.

That same Christmas Oom Albert and Tante Truus from Abbotsford came to our place for the day. Oom Albert was my mother's brother and owned a small garage. They had a daughter my age named Ada, whom I was glad I did not have to see often.

I was only seven that Christmas, and several days later my father told my brothers they could burn the Christmas tree.

"Take Hennie along why don't you," my mother said.

"Aw, she's too little. We'll just have to wait for her, she's so slow."

But my mother persisted, because all of us gone would mean quiet in the house. "Hurry up, Hennie," she said, "put on your things. And don't forget your scarf."

My brothers were waiting for me outside. The air was cold, wet snow was falling, and I was glad for my mittens. I put my hands in my pockets and hunched my shoulders. Leonard, being the oldest, had the honour of carrying the tree. He hoisted the trunk and dragged the tree behind him as if he were a hunter hauling a dead lion by the tail. They started off.

"Hey, where are we going?" I asked.

"Just follow us," Leonard shouted.

I managed to keep up with them a while, but then the snow began to slow me down and I could feel the first bites of cold through my mittens. When my hands began to hurt I took off one mitten and put my fingers in my mouth, surprised at how cold my fingers tasted and how warm my hand felt in my mouth. I thought of the wood stove in the kitchen and how nice it would be to hold my hands to it.

"Hurry up, Hennie!" They stood ahead of me, waiting, the trees dark behind them. Both my hands felt numb.

"I'm cold. How much farther is it?"

"We're almost there, now come on. You shouldn't have come then!"

They started off again, me trailing them. They moved closer to the back of the pasture, then entered the gully where the bush began. The snow had stopped falling. In the trees it was suddenly dark. My pants were wet now just above my boots, the skin irritated where the top of the boot chafed against my leg.

By the time I reached my brothers they had the tree all arranged, pieces of newspaper stuffed under it. Then Leonard held a match to the paper and stepped back. I watched the paper turn brown where the little flame licked, then it caught the first branch and sprang into flame. Immediately the whole tree was ablaze with a crackling roar. I took off my mittens and held out my hands to catch the heat. I could feel the warmth seeping through my pants. The flames spurted high, crackling sharply, the tinsel caught in the branches fluttering in the blaze.

As abruptly as it had roared to life the fire died down, leaving the gully pitch dark. I did not see my brothers beside me and looked around wildly in alarm, all the weight of the trees' blackness suddenly upon me. Then I caught a glimpse of my brothers against the night sky as they disappeared over the top of the gully.

"Hey, hey wait for me!" I scrambled up the steep slope, snow getting into my boots and sleeves, chilling me. When I reached the top I could see my brothers far ahead, running towards the lights of the house in the distance. I ran, then fell, stumbling to catch up to my brothers in the dark, not wanting them to hear me crying with rage.

Especially during those first years my mother found it difficult to adjust to Canada, an ailment my father called by its Dutch name, *heimwee*, which meant longing for home. She would often tell me stories about Holland, about her childhood, how she had started work at sixteen, and how she'd met my father. Or she showed me photographs of relatives caught in still poses, and she would tell me about each one in a soft voice: "That's your Oma, she's 84. And that one is Volkert, who was killed by the Nazis." And it all seemed like another world to me, for unlike my brothers I remembered nothing of Holland.

Because of her *heimwee*, she was unable to do a number of things. Whenever I was over at my friends' places their mothers made next day's lunches after supper, mixing the pat of orange powder through margarine to give it colour, then spreading it on piles of brown bread to be covered with Gouda cheese and Spam and *rookvlees*; they canned beans and applesauce and peaches in the summer, the kitchen steaming with water boiling on the stove, the counter and plastic tablecloth littered with slimy fruit and vegetable pulp; they spent all day Monday pushing the wash, piece by piece, through a wringer washer, hanging the clothes on the line outside in summer and in a dank basement in winter, their hands wet and chapped and red. My mother felt paralyzed to do any of these things. My father and I made our lunches, talking softly if my mother had gone to bed, my brothers also strangely quiet, as if there had been a death in the house. We ate our fruit and vegetables from cans which we bought at the Red and White in town eight miles away, and a woman down the road, an immigrant like ourselves but from some Slavic country, came in once a week to do our wash. My mother had homesickness.

Even during her better times she was able to do only minimal tasks at home, cooking simple and predictably similar meals, and keeping the house reasonably clean, clean enough to suit my father, brothers, and me, but far short of the ideal of order and cleanliness maintained, for instance, by my Tante Truus who, when she visited, seemed almost afraid to sit in a chair. When my mother felt better she sat at the kitchen table writing letters to relatives in Holland, her sharp, pointed handwriting filling the blue airmail paper which she then folded and licked shut to form a neat envelope. I wondered how she always made whatever she wanted to say fit into so prescribed a length, but now I wonder even more just what the letters contained, what portion of those first years she chose to communicate to family back home.

When not writing letters she sat in her maroon velour chair reading one Dutch novel after another which she borrowed from the church's library, keeping the rest of us waiting after the Sunday morning service while she traded in her books, I in the cab of our pickup with my father in deference to my being a girl, my brothers in the back. Occasionally, if my mother felt I would enjoy or profit from a particular novel, she would urge me to read it and I would dutifully begin, but by the end of the week I would not have gotten very far for the novels all seemed to me as drab as the brown shopping bag paper the enterprising church librarian wrapped them in, and I knew my mother would not have the patience to keep the book another week while I finished reading it.

During her worst times she was depressed, sitting by the window for hours at a time simply staring at the trees surrounding our place, looking out at the bush as if its mysterious, shadowed places were a part of her own mind. Her eyes would not blink or move an inch for long periods of time, and even when some distraction in the room drew her attention she turned her head languorously and looked with eyes that were out of focus as if she were staring at something far beyond the walls of the room. She slept much of the day and went to bed shortly after supper.

I wondered at times whether something could be done to make her feel better, although I was afraid my father might consider returning to Holland for her sake. But then I heard a man tell my father that his relatives in Arnhem laughed at him when he returned for a visit because he was still wearing the same suit he wore when he left, and I knew we would stay in Canada. As for me, despite the unsettling effect upon us of my mother's illness, I was convinced we lived in the best of all possible places, and did not see how she could ever long for another, did not see why she could not force herself to feel at home where we lived.

The spring I was eleven she suffered a nervous breakdown. The winter had been unusually long and hard, with snowstorms cooping us up in the house for days. Finally in late March the snow began to melt, turning our dirt road to mud. People stomped their feet on the mat at the back door before taking off their boots. That Saturday was one of those days your body feels sure for the first time that spring has come. My mother had lain in bed for several days, and at supper time I went to her bedroom to see if she wanted anything to eat, but she said nothing. At eight o'clock I went in again to see how she was; she lay on her side, her head under the blanket and her knees drawn up, and when I asked her if she wanted anything she did not respond. I touched her shoulder but she would not answer. The room had been dark for days. I went to tell my father.

"I wonder if something's wrong with Mother. I don't think she's sleeping, but she won't say anything."

My father went to the bedroom and turned on the little light by the bed. "Nel," he said, "Nel." My mother did not move. He lifted the top of the blanket but my mother's hand lay on her temple, shielding her eyes. My father stroked her back, then after some minutes he rose. "I'd better call Rev. Hordyk," he said outside the bedroom.

Rev. Hordyk was there half an hour later. I did not go into the bedroom with them and after a while I heard their voices low in the hall. Then my father called Dr. Weber, who also drove out. After the three of them had been in my mother's room for what seemed a long time I finally heard the door open and I saw my father with his arm around my mother, her suitcase in his hand. She was wearing her housecoat and slippers, taking small shuffling steps. By the door I almost told her she should put on her boots but then my father put down the suitcase and carried her to Dr. Weber's car. Then he came back and told us she would have to go to the hospital and that we should not wait up for him. We all knew "the hospital" was Essendale, a mental institute. I watched the car's red lights go down the road until they were blocked by the trees. Afterwards my brothers and I sat around hardly talking, frightened and bewildered by what had just happened. Finally Leonard said, "We'd better go to bed," and started turning off the lights. In my room I prayed for my mother in Essendale, and thought of the rhyme chanted mockingly by kids at school:

> Rooty-toot-toot, rooty-toot-toot,
> We're the boys from the Institute,
> We're not from Harvard,
> We're not from Yale,
> We're the boys from Essendale!

I could not bear to think of that, and turned on my brothers' castoff radio for company in my loneliness, listening to music until late. The last thing I remembered was the radio transmission broken by rhythmic waves of static. Next morning I woke to popular music that seemed almost sacrilegious for such a serious Sunday.

During the next weeks we shared responsibilities in the house, my father doing the cooking every day after he came home from work so that we didn't eat until late, my brothers trying to be helpful by doing the dishes but having little feel for it, their hands clumsy handling plates and cups, the milk glasses taking on a dull grey film. My father was allowed to see my mother once a week but we were not permitted to come along, and when he came home and we asked whether she was feeling better he said only that Mother was very ill and that it would take her a long time to get well. When May passed, then most of June, I began to long for her to come home and wrote short get-well notes and drew pictures of the house and the barn and the animals for my father to give her. By the end of June, school was over and Karl graduated from grade eight. I wondered what kind of a vacation I would have.

Leonard got his first job that summer, working on a farm, and my father made an arrangement with Billy and Karl that he would pay them so much each for doing odd jobs around the yard, sawing wood, weeding the garden, cleaning the chicken shed. I felt offended that he had not included me, for the jobs certainly did not seem like anything I could not handle just as well as they. He must have felt puzzled what to do with me, reluctant to let me have the run of the place with my mother gone.

The solution, from his point of view, came the day that Tante Truus was over to clean the house. She'd called every week or two to hear if there was any news about my mother and during one conversation told my father she would drive to our house for a day to do some cleaning. I think my father resented the offer but protested only weakly, and several days later Tante Truus drove into our yard. From the trunk of her car she extracted brushes, a broom, several pails, and a handful of rags, as if such things were foreign to our house. I'd felt the weight of her coming and, not wanting her to find the house a total disgrace, had spent the previous day straightening out closets and cupboards and hiding in the basement the objects of certain embarrassment: pans with burnt bottoms, cups with ears broken off, the wooden kitchen chair with wobbly legs, but these things were only cosmetic, I knew, compared with the damage I could not hide—the top of the wood stove caked with black rings, the spilled raspberry juice in the bottom of the refrigerator, the linoleum floors sticky with dirt—which Tante Truus would attack, wondering all the while how things could possibly go so far. Indeed, she spent the day washing, scrubbing, scraping—I assume, for I did not want to be present to witness the humiliation and stayed outside in the yard, watching now and then as she heaved a pail of dirty water into the grass from the back porch.

After supper my father called me into the house to explain that she had invited me to their place in Abbotsford to go berry picking with Ada, perhaps until my mother could come home.

"What do you think?" he said. "Want to?"

I did not feel much like going for I thought my mother might be well soon and didn't want to miss her coming home.

"I'd rather stay here," I said.

"Listen, I think it's better if you go. You'll be lonesome by yourself. Don't worry about us."

I knew what he meant when he said "by yourself," that it might not be pleasant for me to be the only girl there with him and the boys. I wanted to tell him that this was nothing new for me but then, remembering how concerned I had been about the house before my aunt's coming, I was suddenly not sure whether that was the truth.

I packed my suitcase and left in the car with Tante Truus, feeling terribly betrayed by my father, and vowing to be back within two weeks.

It rained the first several days I was at my cousin Ada's, and we did not go berry picking. We hung around the house and spent most of the time talking in her bedroom. Her window looked out on a row of back yards filled with cedar fences soaking wet and swing sets dripping rain. Her bedroom was small and neat, like a motel room awaiting an occupant. She had hung a picture of Paul Anka above her bed and on a small table in the corner stood a fishbowl with two goldfish motionless in the water, their only movement the mechanical stirring of their fins.

Tante Truus was in the kitchen all day canning fruit, and for a while we helped her remove the pits from a crate of cherries. By late afternoon a batch of Mason jars stood on the counter and the air hung redolent with the sweet smell of sugared fruit juice.

At six o'clock Oom Albert came home from the garage. He took off his shirt at the kitchen sink and washed himself there, scrubbing Dutch Cleanser into his hands with a bristle brush. Suntan covered his face and arms and came down in a small V below his throat, the rest of his skin smooth and white like a boiled egg.

"You could leave me some room, Truus," he said in his high voice, removing from the sink some of the bowls my aunt had used in canning. Then he took off his socks and shoes, rolled up the bottom of his pants, and lifted one foot into the sink, washing it with a face cloth. When he finished washing his feet he dried them with a tea towel and sat down with the newspaper.

He'd hardly started reading when he snorted, "Hmm, I see that Tommy Douglas is making an ass of himself again. Him and them socialists. What they need over there in Saskatchewan is a Social Credit government, Truus, like we got here. Bennett would straighten those farmers out pretty fast."

Tante Truus finished setting the table and called us to supper.

Oom Albert put down the paper with a loud rustle. "Come to think of it," he said rising from his chair, "that's the same place Diefenbaker's from. No wonder we got so much unemployment." He sat down. "Well, shall we start?"

I'd no sooner sat down than he began praying in Dutch, his voice a sing-song just like the one Rev. Hordyk used. He asked for a blessing on the food and that my mother be restored to good health and sound mind, then started to ladle steaming potatoes and beans onto his plate, mashing them all together with gravy, turning his plate with quick movements.

Tante Truus shoved a pan towards me. "Come on Hennie, help yourself, *meid.*" After a moment she spoke again. "I hope your father and the boys are all right out there all by themselves." I wondered what she thought went on at our house, "out there" sounding as if my father and brothers were camping out in the wilds.

"Ja," Oom Albert said, "no wonder Nel got lonely, *arme stakkerd.*" It was a phrase I'd heard my father call animals in suffering. "Your father will have to move to town after this, Hennie, so your poor mother can have some company." And he began asking questions about our family, obviously prying in the hope that I would provide incriminating support for his conviction that my father was disgustingly unlike any other decent Dutch immigrant and that some pretty terrible things must therefore be going on at our house. And I, I lied unashamedly, describing how my mother baked pies, re-painted our living room, and made clothes for me.

"Still," Oom Albert said, "I hope your father learns from this."

After supper Ada asked if I felt like reading comic books and I said all right, but the ones she took out of her closet were *True Romance* comic books about beautiful girls who always ended up being jilted, every story concluding with close-ups of their faces with huge tears spilling from the corners of their eyes.

"How old are you gonna be when you get married?" Ada asked me. I sensed by the urgency in her voice how important the question was to her and couldn't tell her I hadn't even thought about it.

"When I graduate from high school I'm gonna get a secretary's job in Vancouver and start saving for a hope chest right away," she said, her voice flat as if all the excitement of her future had been expended in dreaming it up and all that remained now was the mundane reality of fulfillment.

The next days turned hot with the previous days' humidity still heavy in the air and we went berry picking, getting up at five in the morning, reaching the field by six, then crouching in the hot soil picking strawberries until late afternoon, my fingers stained a deep red and my back aching and sunburned. That first day I made three dollars, Ada five.

Tante Truus seemed to think we had done quite well. "Just think," she said, "after several weeks you'll be rich."

The truth was that after several weeks I was ready to go home. I longed for our own house, for the yard with Dief nibbling grass, for a ride through the pasture on Brandy, for my father and the smell of sawmill wood on his clothes, longed even for my brothers.

Then my father called one evening and I could tell from my aunt's response that my mother had been allowed to come home. Then Oom Albert talked to my father, saying "Sure, sure, that's fine." Finally the phone came around to me and my father confirmed that my mother had been released from the hospital. "But listen, Hen," he said, "I think it's better if you stay there a bit yet so it won't be too busy for her right away."

"How long?"

"Let's just say a week or two."

"Two weeks!"

And then I was filled with resentment, resentment toward my father for the implication that it was my presence and not my brothers' that made it too busy for my mother, toward my uncle for his high, hectoring voice, my aunt for her cleanliness, toward Ada for her dullness, resentment toward all of them for standing around the phone so that I was prevented from saying how much I disliked it there and how desperately I longed to come home.

I spent the next few days scheming of ways I could create sympathy towards myself and be allowed to come home. I could fake stomach cramps, have mysterious headaches, eat green apples and have diarrhea.

Then, as it turned out, it was a stupidity, my own dumb stupidity, that allowed me to come home. One of the kids in the neighbourhood had a bow although without arrows, and I set out to teach Ada how to shoot. I cut a maple branch, peeled off the bark with a knife and whittled the head to a point, even made the slot in the tail for the string. I showed Ada how to rest the arrow lightly on her left hand, to pull back the bowstring with the first three fingers, then to release, but the arrow curved through the air, always veering past the target.

"That's one lousy arrow," Ada said.

"Yeah, and I know the reason. It's because it doesn't have any feathers."

But even if we found feathers, how to cut them and glue them to the arrow? It would have to be something other than feathers.

In the basement of Ada's house I found what we needed: pieces of roofing tin. Ada gave me Oom Albert's tin snips and I cut three little parallelograms of tin that, because of the sharpness of their edge, I would be able to push right into the arrow's shaft.

"Let me shoot it first," Ada said.

"No, I'd better try it." I pointed the bow into the air, rested the arrow lightly on my left hand, and pulled back the string, dramatically lowering the bow until the arrow tip pointed at the target.

I did not even feel the tin slice through my hand. But suddenly the blood spurted, welling over my hand, and I felt my thumb hang loose.

Oom Albert raced me to emergency. Afterward he called my father and I was right about the sympathy part. As I was driven home that evening, my hand encased in stiff white bandage, I sat trying to summon whatever strength and bravery I could, strength and bravery I would need to face the certain scorn of my father and brothers for something so dumb it could only have been done by a girl. Never mind. I was going home, home.

The next year my father sold our place and we moved to New Westminster so that my mother could be in the company of more Dutch people. She suffered another nervous breakdown five years later. My father still works in a sawmill on the Fraser River beneath the Queensborough Bridge.

And I have learned some things about myself since then. People often told me at the time that I looked exactly like my mother and this irritated me terribly, convinced as I was that the resemblance was more perceived than real and that people said this to me out of a widespread conspiracy that young girls **ought** to resemble their mothers. I did not wish to look like my mother. I did not like the way she dressed me Sundays in stiff dresses, the large hair ribbon which she liked to put on top of my head, and the old coat of hers from Holland which she had a tailor remodel to fit me. Looking at myself in the mirror now, however, I suspect that not only were people speaking the truth but that now I am beginning to resemble the person she once was, in outward appearance at least, even more. Now capitulation has dulled her eyes, rounded and swollen her face, but when I look at photographs of her as she was in Holland, then I see I have her eyes, bulging slightly beneath eyebrows that seem permanently half-raised as if in constant surprise, eyes that pierce out like those of a startled bird. I have her hair, curly stuff that refuses to do what I want and to whose will I have had to learn to resign myself if I was to live with it at all. And I have the angular features my mother had then, nose, mouth, chin, that suggest both our faces might have been whittled by a sharp knife.

I have never been back to Holland and now, after twenty-three years, I have decided it is time I go. The travel agency in Vancouver has mailed me my ticket, my name and address neatly typed in black on the first page, in progressively fading red carbon through the ticket's waxy pages, pages filled with mysterious numbers and abbreviations I do not understand but which enable me to cross an ocean and, eight hours later, step off in the country which my mother so faithfully, so obsessively for twenty-three years, always considered home.

I am going in order to discover whether the stories she told me of Holland were embellished by time and distance, or whether they were true. I may discover something about her, about myself, and just how much of this story I have told you is, after all, true.

PISCES

The power of the visible
is in the invisible

—Marianne Moore

Baars was so deep in his daydream that his wife had to ask her question three times before he heard her voice. They were driving towards Lake Erie with their twin boys, and what Baars was thinking about was their upcoming week at the lake, and then he certainly felt in good spirits. Lots of sun and water, plus some casual research with fish and algae around Erieau. Through his mind ran the refrain of a song he'd heard on the radio earlier. He found it rather pleasant and sang it to himself over and over:

> *Joy to the world,*
> *All the boys and girls,*
> *Joy to the fishes in the deep blue sea,*
> *Joy to you and me.*

Baars liked that. The song's tone struck him as being entirely appropriate. After all, if the benefit of man's being crown of creation did not extend to the animals, then what **did** it mean? Yes, joy to the fishes of the deep blue sea, all right, even those of Lake Erie, if people would only listen to the voice of science.

It was then Baars finally heard his wife's question, and even so it did not register at first. He was only half aware of her, sitting uncomfortable and heavy with pregnancy on the opposite end of the front seat, when her voice broke his daydream. What motel had he reserved, she wanted to know. What motel indeed? Suddenly

Baars felt as if he had just made a serious miscalculation in an experiment, with his whole graduate class looking on. What motel indeed?

He confessed that he had forgotten to make the reservation.

One hour later they stood at the town's last motel, the red neon sign glowing *No Vacancy* as a bright reminder of Baars' stupidity.

"Try anyway," his wife said, "you never know. Maybe the sign's wrong."

"Fat chance," Baars snorted, taking on a sour look, as if she had just asked him to make a public fool of himself. "This is ridiculous," he said.

"What's ridiculous," her voice snapped from the open car window, "is that you didn't write for reservations, like I suggested."

He stepped into the motel office, was told the sign was indeed correct, and emerged with a scowl on his face. He felt very angry at himself for not having made the reservation, not only for the inconvenience his error now caused, but especially because he had always considered efficient, rational planning his most outstanding trait. He felt both irritated and mystified that it had momentarily deserted him. What had possessed him to forget?

"We've tried all the motels, now what?" Hume wailed from the back seat.

"Maybe we can rent one of the cottages around here," Baars said, hoping to salvage his respect.

"That means we won't have a swimming pool!"

"And what's wrong with having a beach? All you've got here is the whole of Lake Erie!"

"It's polluted," David complained. "My teacher says there's nothin' in it but dead fish."

"Well, your teacher just happens to be wrong. Scientists have been working on it, and I ought to know."

He drove slowly away from the town, away from the resort area. At the first intersection, he saw that the road to the left followed the lake and that it was lined with cottages. He turned onto it.

"Dike Road," David groaned, reading the road sign. "Dike Road. What a hick place."

"Yeah," Hume chimed in, "who wants to spend their vacation on a stupid onion farm." The road was narrow, without a centre white line. On the right the pavement was fringed by a tangle of tall grass and blooming dandelions, the ground dropping off sharply to a broad, water-filled ditch. Beyond the ditch lay fields of black dirt bisected by row after straight row of onions.

Baars dropped the visor above him to shield his eyes from the late afternoon sun. "What do you suggest?" his wife asked, arching her eyebrows.

"Let's just take a look down here," he said, stalling.

On the left, green lawns separated the road from the cottages, a few of which stood farther back shaded by maples and willows and elms. Far beyond Baars saw the keen edge of the lake's horizon slice sharply against the sky. What surprised him, however, was the narrowness of the neck of land between the cottages and the lake, as if half the beach had been cut away. I'd have given myself a bit more room, he thought. Then he saw two cottagers lifting rocks into wire-mesh cages piled on top of each other along the lake shore. Others built walls with sandbags, like the besieged villagers in Holland Baars remembered from the War. So that was it: the lake must have been high. Half a mile farther a row of cottages stood perilously close to the lake, then a number of them had been jarred from their moorings and tossed aside, torn to splintered boards. Waves dashed through the caved-in walls, flinging spray as high as the roofs. Then the road itself veered close to the lake, and water flew over the pavement.

"Gol!" one of the boys shouted as a wave crashed, tossing spume against the windshield.

This is getting close, Baars thought. He drove slowly.

A hundred yards farther on the air smelled suddenly putrid, the car filling with the stench of decay, and after a moment Baars saw why. In a marsh, littered among the spiked reeds and muddied spears of grass, lay the decomposing bodies of hundreds of dead carp.

"Peeyew!" the boys groaned, rolling up their windows.

"Let's turn back," Baars' wife said, closing her eyes and turning away.

"How come they're dead, Dad?" Hume asked.

"High winds must have raised the water level, and when the lake receded the fish were trapped." He turned the car around. When he had almost reached the road leading back to town his wife said, "Maybe you should ask that lady over there if any of these cottages are for rent."

He did not want to do any such thing, but realizing he had little choice he slowed the car. Ahead the motels were full; behind him the sun began to sink lower, reflecting an angry glare in his rear view mirror. The woman was down on her hands and knees weeding a bed of purple zinnias. Her cottage was much larger than the others and was built of white stucco rather than wood siding. On the front lawn geraniums bloomed inside two car tires that had been turned inside out and painted white. Baars stopped the car and stepped out, feeling uncomfortably like a door-to-door salesman.

The woman had seen the car and was waiting on all fours. Her body was huge and she wore a white kerchief tied in two knots that stuck out like horns from her forehead, so that she resembled a bull irritated at being interrupted while feeding.

"Excuse me, ma'am," Baars said, "but could you tell me if any of these cottages are for rent?"

The woman eyed him a moment, then craned her neck to look past him at the car. "How long are you thinking of?" she said.

"Oh, a week, maybe."

She stood up, brushed the hair out of her face with a gloved hand, then slowly removed the gloves, all the while eyeing Baars and the car. She spoke with a European accent, asking him why he wanted a cottage over here rather than a motel in town, and whether the boys were good boys and not destructive. Baars answered, not telling the whole story of the motel but saying they wanted to stay away from the commercialized area. He felt interrogated and wanted to retreat to the car, convinced he had made a mistake. He turned to go.

"Mr. Cragg next door sometimes rents his cottage," the woman said, pointing.

Baars looked at her, then over at the cottage. It was painted white with green shutters and trim. It looked neat enough. He thanked the woman and walked across the lawn, wondering whether he should have walked around it on the road. Ahead of him the sun hung red as a bruised berry in the trees in the west.

Baars pressed the doorbell but no one answered. From inside he heard the broadcast of a baseball game. He tried knocking. Immediately the sound inside was turned down and the door opened. Again Baars wondered whether he had made a mistake. Before him stood an old man whose nose and cheeks were bulbous and red, criss-crossed with dark purple veins. His hair lay greased on his head, the thin front of it pushed forward in a rakish wave. He wore a white T-shirt and beneath it his pants hung low, the belt buckle hidden under a sagging belly.

He agreed to let Baars and his wife look through the cottage. They were satisfied with it and decided to rent it for a week.

"Just give me a sec to move my stuff into the garage," Cragg said. "I've got it all decked out for when I rent out the place."

They spent the evening unpacking the station wagon, Baars carrying suitcases inside where his wife emptied them. Later, after they had put the boys to bed, they sat at the kitchen table. Baars' wife sat straight in her chair, one hand cupped over the top of her protruding stomach.

"Beat?" Baars asked.

"Sort of," she said, then placed her hand over his on the table as if to atone for her snappishness that afternoon. "First the long drive, then the looking for a place." Her sentence trailed off, and they sat silently.

He was in his fourth year at the University of Guelph when they'd married, while she was just a year out of high school. She had worked five years in a bank supporting them while he did graduate studies. They had tried to have children then, when he was finished, but were unsuccessful, and finally the doctor had advised them to adopt. Soon after, they had received the twin boys from the agency. Now, eight years later, she had suddenly become pregnant. She was a good mother but Baars, assuming that the complexity of his research lay beyond her comprehension, shared little of his work with her, and he was aware of her dissatisfaction over how little he seemed to need her.

They had debated whether to have a vacation this summer, what with her pregnancy—her first, after all—and had decided that perhaps a quiet week in a motel by the lake would not prove too strenuous for her. Which made his failure to make the reservation all the more serious, and as it crossed his mind again he was filled anew with embarrassment.

"I think we'll enjoy it here," he said. "The boys will have plenty to do."

She smiled wanly. "You're not going to spend all your time doing research, though, are you?"

"I promise. But there are a few things I want to look at."

Fatigue showed on her face, and she suggested they go to bed.

"I don't think I can sleep yet," he said, "you go ahead. I'll just grab some fresh air a moment and then be right in," and he kissed her.

When he stepped outside he saw Cragg sitting against the garage smoking. Baars sat down on a stump beside him. "Nice evening," he said. He looked up and saw a half a moon in the sky, the dark half faintly visible like a shrivelled and black-green globe of fruit.

"What do you do, Baars?" Cragg asked.

"I'm a biologist. Ph.D. from Guelph."

"How about that. And you decided to come here for your vacation."

"Mostly. I haven't been to this part of the lake for a while, and I thought I'd do some poking around. You know, kill two stones with one bird," and he chuckled, but Cragg did not laugh. "Looks like you've been hit though," he began again.

"I'll tell ya," Cragg said, "she's been nasty. Had us a few good storms this spring. I think the beach is ten foot higher 'n what it was.

Had a willow down there by the dock at one time. Not no more. Snapped right off, like it was a toothpick. You're sittin' on it now. But we been lucky compared with down the road. Care for a beer?"

He disappeared into the garage without waiting for Baars to reply and after a moment came out with two bottles.

"I noticed the people sandbagging," Baars said.

"Won't do no good," Cragg scoffed. "I seen her throw trees like they was nothin', and she don't pay no more attention to us. Best thing for us is to stay out of her way. As far as the water itself is concerned, I suppose it's been gettin' better. Can see bottom now at two feet. And they're back fishin' on it, commercial, I mean."

"It shows you what responsible science can do," Baars said. "Course, it helps that Erie is small. Takes just seven years for it to change its water completely. The other four are bigger so they take much longer."

Cragg seemed duly impressed with this information.

"How about you, Mr. Cragg, what do you do?"

"Call me Don. Me? I'm retired now. Ph.D. from Michigan. Economics."

"You don't say," Baars said. Maybe he had misjudged this Cragg.

"Naw, I'm kiddin' ya. I went to the school a hard knocks. Worked thirty years in the Ford plant in Detroit."

"Are you an American then?" Strange fellow, Cragg.

"Nope. Canadian as hell. From Moose Jaw."

"How did you end up in Detroit?"

"I played hockey. Got a tryout long time ago with the Red Wings."

"I see," Baars said, skeptical now. He did not intend to get hooked twice.

Cragg, however, seemed serious. "That was in the days of Delvecchio and Abel and them boys, though. No way I was going to crack that lineup, not before expansion. Somehow I never left Detroit. Played some industrial hockey, bought the cottage in the meantime, then when the wife died four years ago I decided to sell the place in Detroit and live here. How about you, sounds like you got an accent—German?"

Baars laughed. "No, Dutch."

"Well, I had you figured wrong then. Ever since the War I can't stand them Germans. But I got to introduce you to Thelma next door. She's Belgian. Same thing, right?"

"Almost. Actually, I met her already. She's the one who told me about your place."

"Mmm, wonder what made her do that. Usually she's pretty leery of me gettin' someone in here. Bit of a kook, if you ask me. Inta horoscopes and ouija boards and all that. You believe in that?"

Baars laughed again. "Wouldn't look too good for a scientist, would it." He felt the evening chill and rose to go. "Thanks for the beer."

"That's O.K. Maybe tomorra your boys can get some fishin' in. You fish?"

"A little."

"Tell ya what. One a these days I'll take ya out in my boat and we'll catch us a mess of perch. You cut yours open and look inside. I'd rather eat mine!"

"O.K., Don," he laughed. "See you tomorrow."

Despite the boys' earlier fears, Baars saw that they had a good time at the lake. They found that the ditch across the road contained small gold carp and spent hours trying to catch them. David fashioned a net from some wire and netting, stationed himself at a narrow point in the ditch, and had Hume try to herd the carp toward him, but the fish were elusive, darting back in a flash of gold. Cragg took the boys to the onion farm to find worms under logs, then pointed out some good fishing spots, teaching them how to cast into the lake. Baars watched, envious of Cragg's easy manner with the boys, glad, however, that it freed him to do some research. He stopped in at the commercial fishery in town to see what fish were now being caught and left with some skin tissues of perch and whitefish. He collected some water samples along the lake shore, which he would check for concentration of blue-green algae.

He felt in his element then. The last few years he had become somewhat disenchanted with teaching, wondering whether he should quit and do research for industry. Students weren't the same anymore. Drugs, science fiction, Zen this and that—just a bunch of mystics. The trouble with them was that they had no appreciation for two thousand years of Western culture.

Cragg, however, seemed an interested pupil. "So that's what causes that, eh?" he said when Baars explained the reason for the foam on the beach. "You know I've seen the layer of scum in the middle of the lake to be a mile wide? And so thick I swear you could of walked right there on the water. How'd that be for a trick! But you fellas think you can fix all that, huh?"

"We can go a long way," Baars said. "But unless we stop dumping toxic wastes and using mercury for fungicide, we're going to have a hard time." He had said the words often. Classes at the university, speeches to service clubs and church groups, at all of them he had spread his view of a scientific approach to the environment. He felt proud knowing that man possessed the knowledge to improve his world, and that science stood in the forefront of this progress.

His words didn't have the effect on Cragg that he had hoped, however. "You're way beyond me already," Cragg chuckled. "Toxic wastes and funga-whatnots—I'll leave that up to you boys. The only mercury I know is the kind with four wheels on it. Hell, I've paid my dues. All I want's my pension from Ford and I'm happy." He rose from the willow stump. "I'll let you fellas clean up the world. Wanna beer?"

Baars was reading *The Journal of Marine Biology* under the parasol of the picnic table, oblivious to his wife sunning in a lawn chair to his left. A white summer top hung taut over her stomach, and the skin of her arms and shoulders glistened under a coating of baby oil.

"What time is it, dear?" she asked.

Baars glanced at his watch. "Pretty well three o'clock," he said.

"Oh, we've got to get ready then. I forgot to mention it to you, but Thelma asked us over for a cold drink this afternoon."

Baars looked at her. "I wish you would have checked with me first," he said. He had hoped to avoid Thelma. He felt she was a suspicious old woman. He had noticed her watching him from her window as he worked with his samples. His mind had been nagged, moreover, by the notion that she was not only unpleasant but even, perhaps—well, sinister. It was something Cragg had said about her.

"Oh come on, don't be so anti-social," his wife said, struggling to rise from her chair. "She's a very nice lady. Besides, I'm about ready for a cold drink."

So was Baars, but it did not make him feel any better as they walked over.

Thelma met them at the door, wearing a flowing silky dress with a pattern of turquoise flowers, a dress which Baars thought was rather low-cut for her age. A kerchief of the same material tied her hair and flowed down her back. Thin golden hoops dangled from her ears to her shoulders.

"It's so nice to have you two stop by," she sang, ushering them in.

The living room they stepped into was cool, with a slight breeze from the lake rustling the print curtains, but Baars felt uneasy. The walls were painted a deep blue and in the room hung a strange odour which he could not identify. It wasn't the zinnias or chrysanthemums or asters which stood in vases everywhere; the smell was more like incense, and Baars felt as if he had just stepped into an alien Eastern shrine. He wished he were back in his white lab with its familiar formaldehyde smell.

"Please sit down," Thelma said. "Would you like a lime and vodka?"

"Oh, that would be nice," Baars' wife said.

Baars could tell by its interior finish that the house was more than a summer cottage. The smooth blue walls and gold carpeted floor gave an air of permanence and solidity, unlike Cragg's cottage with its white-washed, bare stud walls and linoleum-covered, sloping floors.

"Well here we are," Thelma crowed as she glided in carrying a tray with three tall glasses and a dish of chocolate candies.

"Your place is nicely built," Baars said. "Looks like it's been here a while."

"Why thank you. My father built it a long time ago. Actually, it was the first house on Dike Road. Isn't it a beautiful setting?"

Baars' wife said it looked lovely.

"I'm afraid the area has deteriorated terribly the last little while, though," Thelma said. "People are building just any kind of cottages now, it's such a shame. And everything in town has become so commercialized, and the black folks coming from Detroit, fishing everywhere—I know we Tauruses are terribly possessive, but . . . Anyway, I hope you're all enjoying your stay?"

"Yes, it's turned out very well," Baars' wife said, "although I was worried for a while, not being able to get a motel," and she glanced at her husband. Baars looked straight ahead.

"You're a biologist I take it, Mr. Baars, the things I see you doing around the lake. Have you found what you came for?"

"Oh, I've just been doing some very informal things," he said.

"Well I just think it's dreadful what they've done to the lake," Thelma said. "And they tell me now that if someone throws a match into the Detroit river it'll actually burn. Can you imagine that?"

Baars' wife said she could not, and what were things coming to.

But Baars thought it time to set things straight, and started into his speech about toxic wastes and mercury in fungicide when Thelma interrupted him.

"But isn't it just a band-aid solution in the long run, Mr. Baars? I agree with you about not using our rivers and lakes as convenient garbage dumps, but **why** do we do it?"

Baars shrugged. "Mass carelessness."

Thelma shook her head. "I think it goes much deeper. I think it's because we've reduced reality to being nothing more than physical, giving us license to plunder."

"Granted," said Baars, "our materialism gets pretty crass—"

"That's not what I mean, Mr. Baars," Thelma broke in. "I'm talking about environmental rape."

"Oh, I don't know if it's as drastic as all that. If it's true what you're saying, that means we'd have to change the whole North American pattern of science and industry, and I—"

"That's **precisely** what I'm saying," Thelma urged. "Listen, we conscript boy scouts to comb the medians of our highways to pick up beer cans, but the fact is we produce them faster than all the boy scouts in the world combined can pick them up!"

Baars shifted uncomfortably in his seat. "I don't know," he said, "it just seems to me you're overstating it. There's been some irresponsible things done to our lakes by industry and agriculture, granted, but surely the way to remedy that is to apply some equally responsible and enlightened science."

"The kind that denies that nature is spiritual, I suppose."

"But what else can we do? Those are separate realms. What we see is what there is."

"But what do we choose to see?"

"Hard cold reality."

"That's all?"

"With our five senses, yes."

"Mr. Baars," Thelma said slowly, "that there's more to reality than what **you** see means only that you've shrivelled your vision, and that makes you no different from our friend Cragg. Are you an Aquarius by the way?"

Baars had expected the topic, but the question irritated him with its suddenness. "I'm sorry," he said curtly, "but I have no idea."

"Well, when's your birthday?"

There she goes interrogating again, Baars thought, not wanting to answer. "Early March," he said hoping his reply would be sufficiently vague.

"Pisces, then."

"For what it's worth."

"Oh, this drink is so refreshing!" Baars' wife exulted, putting down her glass.

"In that case, let me get us all another," Thelma said, gathering the empty glasses. She flowed to the kitchen in a rustle of silk.

Baars' wife turned to him when Thelma was gone. "Don't you get us into an argument now!" she hissed into his ear, but he only glared at her accusingly, as if to say, "**You're** the one who got us here!"

Thelma returned with their drinks and the visit turned exactly into what Baars was afraid it would. Thelma continued her assault. Baars knew there was no hope of returning the conversation to mere pleasantries, and after a trying hour he left with his wife. It bothered him that Thelma had seemed to enjoy the visit.

Cragg threaded his hook through a dew worm the next day, his fingers slimy with the mucus the worm secreted as the steel barb punctured its body. "Hell," he said, "just think of the number of people who'd lose jobs in the auto industry alone, not to mention rubber and petroleum and steel."

Baars watched his bobber roll and toss twenty feet away with the swell of the waves. "That's exactly what I told her," he said.

"Shows you what happens when you let women run the world," Cragg said.

Baars looked at Cragg holding his rod with his elbows out, arms ready, as if something were playing with the bait. He glanced at the bobber and saw it sink, and Cragg gave his rod a strong upward sweep. It bent toward the water in a slight bow, jerking slightly as Cragg reeled in fast. "Whatever it is, it isn't very big," he said.

"Do you want the net?"

"Naw, I won't need it."

Then Baars saw the yellow shape of the fish as it glimmered near the surface.

"Lousy small perch," Cragg muttered as he lifted the fish out of the water. He let it crash into the boat and the perch landed on its back, white belly writhing, until it righted itself. Cragg took a knife out of his tacklebox, placed his foot on the fish's back, and drove the knifepoint through the top of its head. Baars winced as he heard the crunch of steel slicing through the cartilage. The perch flopped twice and lay still.

"Let's see what he did with my hook," Cragg said. He squeezed at the gills to open the mouth and looked inside. "Wouldn't you know it," he said, "happens all the time with these little buggers. Took it right down inside his bloody craw." He took the knife again, cut the corners of the fish's mouth, and sliced away the slimy flesh of the throat until the knifepoint reached the hook deep in the fish and cut it free. Blood dripped through Cragg's fingers. He threw the perch overboard and it landed with a slight splash, sending water circles widening, then it floated away upside down, creamy belly showing. "Can't stand those dinky ones," Cragg said. He reached over the side of the boat and washed his hands of the blood. Baars saw the perch's scales leave his hands and, catching the sun, float like pearls through the green water.

Baars did not feel like fishing anymore. Tomorrow would be their last day at the lake. Strange: for a man who had just had a vacation, he felt in desperate need of one. At least his boys had seemed to enjoy themselves. But on their own, without him. Cragg had seemed to engage their interest all right. When they got home he'd have to spend more time with the boys, playing—what? He realized with dismay that he hardly knew what games they played. Baseball and football, probably, and then he felt how little his own childhood in Holland, with its emphasis on soccer and gymnastics, had prepared him to play with the boys at their games.

And his wife, what kind of a week had she had? It struck him how little he really knew of her world, too, and then he felt suddenly alone. Or empty, as if an old friend had died and no new intimate had yet filled the void. He'd experienced the same feeling once after a conference in Montreal at which he had met a woman biologist with whom he'd had a number of animated conversations, and as he flew home he'd had the feeling that someone very close to him had died.

Monday he would be back in the lab. Perhaps the water samples and fish tissues he'd collected might produce some interesting results, but as he thought about it he felt no hurry to check them in the lab. Perhaps the familiar surroundings would help and he'd again be in the mood.

Perhaps, perhaps. No, he knew it was more than that, more than a passing funk caused by a week that failed to measure up to his expectations. It was more as if a long-held hypothesis had suddenly been found to be false, and years of work had come to nothing. He would have to think things through again. Or had the friend not died after all? Hang that Thelma!

He felt cold then and noticed that the lake lay in shadow, but when he looked toward the shoreline half a mile away he saw that just before the beach the sunlight began again, the water turning lighter green in a sharp line. The white cottages, too, stood in bright sunlight against the trees, warm and inviting.

He did not feel like waiting for the cloud to pass. "How many did we catch, Don?" he asked.

"About a dozen. Just enough for a fish fry."

"What do you say we call it a day."

"O.K. by me. It's too late in the afternoon now anyway."

They started reeling in their lines, Baars quickly so, his bobber skipping across the water in quick little spurts.

All at once it sank, and had it not been for the total deadness on the end of the line Baars might have thought he had a strike. "I'm snagged, Don," he said.

"Couldn't be. You weren't anywhere near the bottom."

"Must be some debris just below the surface. I'll see if I can work it loose," and he pulled the line taut.

"Don't break it, though," Cragg cautioned. "I'll row us there and have a look."

Baars continued yanking at the line, the rod bending in a sharp arc. Afraid to break the rod, he placed it in the boat, then he stood up and took the line in his hand, pulling hard, stretching the nylon like elastic.

"Better sit down," Cragg said.

Suddenly the hook broke free. The line flew through the air with a snap, and the hook struck Baars on the bare chest. Hands flying to the stinging pain, he lost his balance, struck his tacklebox with his right foot, and lurched backward out of the boat.

He was not a good swimmer. He lost sense of where he was, sinking backwards, and as the water closed over him with a cold shock, he felt a sense of utter darkness and he was sure he was lost. Then, as he struggled to right himself in the water, he heard a moan as of a woman giving birth, and at that moment was revealed to him the groan of the creation in its bondage to decay.

He did not drown. He wrestled with the water until he broke loose, and as his head hit the surface, Cragg was there to haul him out.

"I did hear it!" Baars shouted, as if Cragg might not believe him. "It wasn't in my head. I actually heard the voice!"

"What voice?" Cragg said, "I didn't hear no voice. Listen, everything's all right, you're safe now."

EASTER LILY

Terry leaned toward the mirror, chin pushed out, to catch the light on his face as he shaved. Every morning he stroked the blade carefully into the cleft of his chin but he never managed to reach the stubble inside, which hid deep as stamens inside the petals of a flower. As the blade rasped across his skin he cut himself and then he was angry, for his chin was covered with red nicks from other days.

He stared into the mirror. His eyes were set deep beneath a jutting forehead and bushy eyebrows. His nose was flat instead of fine-boned, his lips thick. Pocks scarred his cheeks, while the stubble in his chin always made his face look unkempt. He did not think the girls in the greenhouse found him handsome—but he knew he was strong, for the boss often told him so.

He wondered if the gross image staring back at him had anything to do with his not being smart, like the girls. Sometimes they teased him, "Count to ten for us, Terry," knowing that he couldn't. But he knew he was smarter than some of the people he saw here on the grounds, like the ones who all had puffy faces. They lived in another building and were not allowed to leave for work every day as he could. Which reminded him: when the big hand was at the top of the dial he had to be by the highway or the boss would be angry.

.   .   .

As he sped over pavement broken now with the coming of April the empty bedding flats in the back of the van rattled. Traffic was again heavy, and getting worse, not only in the city but also out here. Was it worth it to employ Terry and to have to pick him up every morning? Well, it didn't take that long. And the kid did work

91

hard, he had to admit. Besides, some things were just not to be measured in dollars and cents—wasn't it his moral duty? The job was suited exactly for that kind of person: just required some muscles, not too much thinking . . . And look at the money he was saving over hiring a regular man. The kid got along well with the girls, too.

.   .   .

Irene's mother finally had to go to her room to wake her after calling three times. Grudgingly she crawled out of bed. If only she didn't have to work again all day. What a way to spend her spring vacation. But then, it did give her some spending money, and at least Janet and Coby would be there again.

She turned on the radio by her bed and the music broke the morning silence. What should she wear today? The greenhouse would be hot, as usual. The white sleeveless blouse and green shorts would do.

She hurried her breakfast. Thank goodness it was Friday. Last day of work—and a date tonight with Kenny Hiemstra! First, dinner at a Chinese restaurant, then a movie downtown.

> *She is wearing a white formal, Kenny a blue suit. They follow the long red gown of the hostess as she escorts them to their table. Kenny pulls out her chair for her, then sits down. The table is covered with a deep red cloth and stands by a window overlooking the bay. Sailboats lie moored against the dock, white hulls bobbing in the water. Beyond the bay a park stretches in the distance, the first white blossoms and lacework of pale green leaves appearing in the trees. They dine on roast duck and sparkling rosé.*

"Irene! Come on now! You'll be late and Dad will be angry."

She stuffed the last piece of toast into her mouth and jumped to her feet, bumping the table and knocking a teacup to the floor. It shattered, the broken ear lying beside the pieces like an accusing question mark.

.   .   .

In the fields to his right, banks of early morning fog hung low. The boss drove quickly; the wheels of the van bounced violently over the broken pavement.

"Is Irene going to be working again today?" he asked, the rattle of the empty bedding slats almost drowning out his question.

"Ja, it's a busy time."

The boss spoke funny, he thought, everything short and chopped off, the words all hard and scratchy like a clipped hedge. He knew that because he was not smart his own words came out slow, but the boss talked funny because he came from Holland. Sometimes Terry couldn't figure out what the boss was saying but then he would not ask the boss to repeat it or else he would seem dumb. Besides, he knew mostly what to do anyway.

This morning the boss spoke only when asked a question. Terry guessed it was because he had things on his mind, and then he understood. Sometimes he had that too, but with him it was when someone had made him angry. Then he would clam up but inside he wanted to strike out at whoever had bothered him.

He liked the boss. Most of the time he was friendly and good to him. The boss had one habit, though, which bothered him. The boss would pull up to a red light and then say, "Well, Terry, looks like we'll have to wait, eh?" Or if it started to rain he would say, "Think it's starting to rain, Terry?" Or when they were unloading bags of peat moss from the van and two bags were left, the boss would say, "Well, looks like only two bags left, eh Terry." He didn't like the way the boss always said these things, as if he couldn't figure them out for himself. After all, he wasn't just a kid. He was 26!

.   .   .

When Irene walked into the greenhouse Janet and Coby were already there, sitting silent at the lunch table with their chins in their hands and staring out at nothing in particular.

"Cheer up," she said, "last day, remember?" but as she looked at the bright beds of flowers beyond the girls, her eyes hurt. It was too early in the morning for so much colour. Then she heard the crunching of tires on the gravel driveway outside and she knew it was her father with Terry. Two truck doors slammed almost simultaneously.

"Might as well face the music," she sighed. That reminded her. She walked to the conveyer belt, reached up to the radio on the shelf, and turned the knob. The music fell over her like soft rain.

.   .   .

Terry loved the tropical smell of the greenhouse every morning. The sweet scent of blossoms, the good musty smell of moist peat, the warm humid air—it was like a fairyland.

The girls stood by the belt, waiting for him. He smiled, then realized suddenly they could do nothing until he provided them with flats and, flushed with the importance of his job, he hurried to the peat bin. He poured the peat into the bin from large plastic bags, then he filled the flats and placed them on the belt. He pushed them slowly through the water spray until they reached the girls.

.   .   .

Petunias this morning. Yesterday marigolds, the day before begonias. She reached for a new flat from the belt, broke off a clump of petunias from the seeding flat, and separated the clump into single shoots. She took the short piece of dowel with the pointed end and rapidly punched holes into the peat, six holes in each tray. Then she inserted the seedlings and pinched shut the hole. Clump after clump, flat after flat.

The air in the greenhouse was hot and humid, as if it were late afternoon, but the dull feeling behind her eyes told her it was still early morning. Too early even to talk, the boredom broken only by the radio. The realization that today was Friday ran through her head as insistent as the beat of the music, and gradually she began to feel as if she were on the verge of some great joy.

> *He drops her off in front of the lobby, then parks the car. As he buys the tickets she stands by demurely. Placing his hand in the small of her back, he escorts her into the theatre. A deep red curtain hangs in front of the screen. They chat animatedly while waiting for the movie to begin. Finally the red curtain lifts. The movie is everything she had hoped. The ending makes her cry, and when Kenny looks at her she laughs with embarrassment through her tears.*

.   .   .

Terry looked at the girls as he filled the flats with peat. They had bantered back and forth this week, then teased him the last two days, and he had enjoyed the attention. He'd miss them next week when he and the boss were alone again. He had not been able to

answer their teasing. His tongue had felt chained inside his mouth
and he wished he could be as quick as they.

So he had spoken as little as possible to them, letting them do the
talking. But in his mind he had felt a secret pleasure at seeing them
his own way. Coby was stubby and low to the ground, like a red
begonia with her splotchy red skin. Janet stood taller, lanky, her
hair long and blond, like a yellow snapdragon. He liked the word,
snapdragon. Like some mean animal, but only in a story. Irene,
though, was an easter lily. The soft white of her neck not yet tanned
by sun was the blush of green along the lily's bloom, then her lips
opened like the blossom of the lily. Open and soft.

.   .   .

"I just can't **wait** to have you tell us all about it," Coby gushed.

"Yeah, you just don't know how lucky you are," Janet said.

"Well, you'll all just have to wait until Sunday after church, I'm
afraid. Then I'll give you a—play by play of the action," Irene said,
fluttering her eyebrows. Then she glowered darkly, pushed her
tongue behind her lower lip, and squeezed her chin into a cleft. They
looked at Terry and laughed.

"I don't see how you can be so **calm** about it and everything,"
Coby said, eyes wide. "I'd be swinging from the water pipes," and
she looked up.

"Naw, too hot to handle," Janet smirked. "Like a certain girl I
know."

Irene felt flattered by the fervour of their envy. Then she saw
Terry staring at her with dull eyes, jaw hanging loose. "What are
you looking at?" she said, offended, and he turned away with an
embarrassed grin. Then she called to him, "Terry, can you come
here a minute?" He walked over from the peat bin. "Terry, I've just
got to go to the bathroom, can you take my place a sec?"

He nodded and she patted him on the arm. "Thanks, Terry,
you're a darling." The girls giggled behind her.

She walked to the bathroom, lit a cigarette, and stared at herself
in the mirror. She decided she liked her face but her figure needed
something yet.

> *She takes off her blouse and shorts, her bra and panties,
> and throws them into a corner. When she turns on the hot
> water for the tub it shoots from the faucet in a solid jet,
> pounding into the tub. Steam billows into the air. Then
> she looks up and down her figure in the mirror but the*

*steam roiling in the air clouds the glass and her body
fades into the mist. She steps into the tub gingerly, then
eases in with her bottom. The hot water brings goose
pimples to her arms. She slides in gradually until the
water reaches her neck. Her face flushes and perspiration
breaks out on her forehead. She looks along the length of
her body under the water and likes the way it glimmers
whitely.*

.   .   .

He didn't know the petunia shoots were this small and fragile. He
touched them gently as if they were the tresses of a girl he loved. It
took him a long time to separate the clumps into individual shoots.
His hands were too strong and some stems snapped, the head of the
seedling hanging down. After labouring at several clumps he was
afraid he would snap more stems, and he decided just to put half
clumps into every hole. He looked at Janet and Coby beside him
and marvelled at how fast they punched holes into the peat at just
the right places. They snickered as they watched him. He wished
Irene would get back. She'd been gone a long time.

.   .   .

He stood admiring the greenhouse. The neatness of everything!
Cement walks rather than dirt paths, pea gravel beds for the flats to
rest on, overhead sprinklers, and everything green and white and
red. A showcase. His brothers in Holland would be proud.

He strolled to his pride, the easter lilies. He counted them again,
four long rows, fifteen to a row, as if the exact number confirmed
their shimmering beauty. The blooms rose up in slender petals of
pale green, then opened forth in trumpets of white blossoms. And
orders for every one of them. Monday they would go out.

He looked at the girls and saw that the belt behind them was full.
He would have to load the dolly and bring the flats to their bed. He
walked over, then saw shoots still in clumps, others with snapped
stems. He stomped over to the girls.

"Who did these! Which one of you girls did these!"

The girls looked at Irene. "Daddy, I had to go a minute, and Terry
said he'd fill in for me."

He turned to the peat bin. "Terry! You know that's not part of
your job! I want you to keep the peat bin full and that's **all** I want
you to do. Understand?"

.   .   .

Better not try that again. The idiot **would** have to mess things up.
And still a whole thirty minutes till coffee break.

.   .   .

He wasn't trying to hurt the seedlings! Irene asked him to help.
And it wasn't her fault either—she had to go to the bathroom.
Better just stick to your job, just work at doing it right.

Beyond the girls the flats stood in large rectangles within the
borders of cement walks. A plastic name marker was stuck into
each of the flats, forming perfectly straight lines, their symmetry
like the straight rows of headstones in the cemetery he could see
from the window of his room.

.   .   .

He should go now. The girls could keep going with Terry, and
that would give him the rest of the morning for deliveries.

"Coffee time!"

"Irene," he said when they were seated, "I'm going now for a
while. Just keep working on the petunias, and if you get that far you
can start on the coleus. I'll be back about lunchtime."

"O.K., Daddy, we'll take care of things."

.   .   .

Terry sat by the peat bin eating a sandwich, watching the girls
laughing among themselves. Begonia sat cross-legged on the floor.
Snapdragon sat on a stool, tall and thin, while Easter Lily lounged in
a captain's chair from her father's office. They munched at their
snacks. The boss once told him there were flowers that ate things.
He wondered if the girls were laughing at him.

.   .   .

She liked it when her father was gone. Just more relaxed. She
reached up and turned up the volume of the radio.

"I betcha all the girls fight over him," Irene said looking at Terry,
loud so that he could hear.

"Naw," Coby snorted, "they probably don't even have girls
there."

"Course they do dummy," Janet said. "It's what you call your basic co-educational institution."

That Janet, she was all right. "Come on, Terry, tell us, how many girlfriends have you got?"

He just sat there by the peat bin with a grin on his face, looking down at his hands. But, she wondered, do those people have feelings like that too? Do they, you know, do it at all? The thought romped teasingly in and out of her mind.

> *Twenty dollars Kenny has spent on her, and of course a girl must show her gratitude. She props her sweater behind her against the car door and slides slowly back, like easing down into a hot tub. But when she opens her eyes a strange thing has happened. It is not Kenny Hiemstra in the car with her but Terry, his hand caressing her back, her shoulders, her arm. His hand rests guilefully on her stomach a moment, and she knows what is coming. His hand moves to her breast, cupping it gently, and she lets him, afraid that he might feel the pounding of her heart.*

She nudged Janet with her elbow, then shouted, "Hey Terry, come on now, you don't have to be embarrassed to tell us."

He grinned again, thick lips curving wetly over his teeth. He looked up, was about to speak, then looked down and mumbled, "I don't have a girlfriend."

"Aw go on," Janet guffawed.

"Yeah, stop kidding us," Coby said.

"I believe him!" Irene said. "Terry wouldn't lie to us, would you Terry. I'll tell you what. One of **us** has to be his girlfriend then. Coby, you?"

"Yucch, not me!"

"Janet, you?"

"No way, Ralph."

"Then it's gotta be me, I guess." She sashayed to Terry, planted a kiss on his cheek, and said, "Terry, I'll be your girl. Now that we're going steady, where will you take me for a date?"

.   .   .

He said nothing. He felt giddy with what was happening, but also scared. Like the outing when he had climbed a rock face steeper than he had ever climbed before, and it was either fall off or keep going to the top. But the girls had placed him on this mountain, and it was up to them to get him off.

.   .   .

"Well, since we love each other we should get married, right?"
Irene ran to a green can holding a dozen white daisies, took them
out, shook off the water, and wove the daisies into a wreath which
she placed on his head. Then she ran to the office and returned with
an old grey suit coat of her father's. When she put it on Terry it hung
halfway to his knees. From beneath the peat bin she took the
broken-off handle of a shovel and put it into his right hand. "You're
ready," she said, "now me!" She took a long white smock hanging
from a nail, put it on over her blouse and shorts, then in her left
hand took a bouquet of white carnations. Her other hand she placed
in his arm. "Now, music!"

"*Here comes the bride*," the girls sang, very solemnly, and Irene
promenaded down the cement walk. Terry shambled beside her,
hopelessly out of rhythm. "*All fat and wide*," the girls sang, then
their voices rose in shrill crescendo, "*Slipped on a banana peel and
went for a ride!*" and the song broke into gales of laughter.

.   .   .

It's a game, he told himself. They have let him play with them.
Then Irene kissed him on the cheek. "Something to remember me
by," she whispered. For safety he shuffled back to the familiarity of
his peat bin.

"What comes **after** the wedding, Terry?" Janet asked in sing-
songy voice. He was not sure what she wanted. What answer was
she after? He shrugged his shoulders.

"The **honey**moon, dum—the **honey**moon. Do you know what a
honeymoon is?" He knew, but which words would explain it?
Janet's voice came again, singing "What do you do on a honeymoon,
Terry?" He did not want to say but her voice would persist, he
knew, until he had said what she wanted. "You take a trip," he
blurted, and the girls screamed in laughter. He laughed too, unsure
whether or not he had made a joke. But Janet didn't stop. She asked
again, "What do you **do** on a honeymoon, Terry?" He couldn't say
it, not to a girl. He looked slyly out of the corners of his eyes and
said, "**You** know," and again the girls laughed.

.   .   .

But inside, Irene didn't laugh. The fantasy had been hers, tantalizing and pure because it was her own, and now Janet had intruded and brought it out into the open, where it seemed suddenly vulgar.

"Come on, guys," she said, "we better get back to work."

The clock said ten to twelve. The red second hand circled slowly. It had been a long morning, a long week, and she was tired. Still a whole afternoon, too, before he would come to pick her up.

The petunia shoots began to irritate her. She no longer had the patience to separate them carefully. She pulled off leaves and snapped stems. She pushed clumps of shoots into each hole. What the heck. Only ten more minutes anyway, then lunch at least. The belt of flats behind her began to back up. "Hey Terry, how about makin' some room for us," she hollered. He came over, started to place the flats on the dolly, then noticed her careless work.

"You're not supposed to do this to them," he said.

Then it all came together: her tiredness, her resentment, her self-disgust, and she turned to Terry and hissed, "Yeah, I guess you should know," then shrill as a trumpet, "you **idiot!**"

. . .

It was the one word he could not take, for it struck at what he knew to be his affliction. He retreated to the peat bin, wounded. He couldn't understand the reason for the sudden change in her. Dug into the peat, his hands clenched into fists. In his mind swirled a mad riot of colour, red, purple, blue, with jagged stabs of white.

. . .

The boss stepped into the greenhouse, anxious to see his lilies again, when instead he saw Terry wearing his old coat and a daisy chain around his head. "What's going on?" he said.

"Oh, just a game we were playing," Irene said.

"But I'm not paying you to play games."

"Well, we did what you told us to do."

"Let's go look once." He walked over. Not that many flats, but it would do—then, *pot verdikkie!* More sloppy flats!

"Irene! Who did these!"

Irene was silent a moment, then she pointed her dowel at Terry and wailed, "I told him he wasn't supposed to do any, but he went ahead and did it anyway!"

"Terry—come here! And take off those—dumb flowers! I thought

I told you not to touch the seedlings! Can't you listen?"

.   .   .

He wanted to protest his innocence, to scream "I didn't do it!" but his mouth just gaped open stupidly and no words came.

"Go ahead and have your lunch now," the boss said.

He stumbled to his lunch pail, took it off the shelf, and sat down with it on a stool by the peat bin.

It was **all** a joke! and he the goat! All this **lovey** stuff. It wasn't right. It had to be set right!

He reached under the peat bin and took out the broken shovel handle, its weight good and heavy in his hands. He started toward the girls, raised the shovel handle and swung it viciously, and the head of the lily sailed through the air. It felt good and he swung again. And again. His breath came more quickly now as the lily heads flew to the floor one by one, the boss hollering far away in the office, "Hey! **Hey!**" and then he was crying as he kept swinging the shovel handle, beheading the lilies so that the splintered stems careened at crazy angles, their necks splayed, and the ground was strewn with white blossoms. Then the boss was rushing at him and he was knocked to the cement floor, his arms pinned against his sides, his breath coming out in heaves, and he knew he had done something terrible. All he kept thinking was that he had not wanted to hurt her but that she had asked for it and that she had it coming.

CLOWN

It was still two hours before the crowds would start filing in through the turnstiles, only ten in the morning but the day already scorching hot, so the kid joined some of the others sitting under the red and yellow striped awning of Jolly Velma's trailer, Jolly Velma panting in her special reinforced chair while the sun reflected in the chrome grille of one of Bustad's trucks nearby with the glare of an acetylene torch, shining from a sky so turquoise it looked as if a child might have coloured it with a crayon.

"I do b'lieve heat's worse for us fat ladies," Jolly Velma sighed, the words rolling slowly from the wet folds of her mouth that reminded the kid of the opening of a ketchup bottle. She daubed at her forehead with a handkerchief, then began waving an ivory-handled fan in front of her face, stirring her thin peroxide hair. The flesh of her arm swung like a water-filled balloon.

"When are you going to get yourself some air-conditioning so's the rest of us won't have to roast, Velma?" Amos the Tattooed Man said. He sat on an overturned Coca-Cola case and wore only a pair of shorts, his body a scrollwork of purple-blue lines from the neck down. A gold ring an inch in diameter hung from his pierced left nipple.

"Yep, harder on us fat ladies," Jolly Velma said again, as if struck by the profundity of this statement. The kid knew she would have worn nothing too, like Amos, if she could have gotten away with it. As it was, a white cotton dress hung on the bulk of her body like a bedsheet draped over a giant mound of rising bread dough.

"Well, you pay for your sins, Velma," Maxine the World's Most Abundant Girl said, arching her copper pencilled eyebrows.

"Maxine honey," Jolly Velma answered, "God **created** my mama a fat lady, bless her soul, but I've got to **work** at bein' what I am, and there ain't no sin in that," and she resumed fanning herself, jewels of sweat running down the bulges of her skin.

The kid was feeling the heat too and knew the afternoon and evening would get hotter still. But he felt good. He was where he wanted to be and maybe today Bustad would let him work a game on the midway rather than one of the rides where there was no shade and time dragged by. He considered himself pretty lucky to be sitting here listening to these folks other people had to pay good money just to have a look at.

On his right, Rufus the dunking machine clown sat drinking from a case of beer. Rufus had been with the carnival just a short time and had taken to fortifying himself with Canadian Club before, during, and after each day's session with the dunking machine — "Keeps my insides warm in that water," he said — but on hot days like today he resorted to beer. Bustad didn't like anyone drinking too close to opening time and he'd threatened several times to fire Rufus if it ever affected him on the job.

Beside Rufus, Septima the World's Tiniest Human sat on a small velvet chair and, except for her grizzled face, looked as if both she and the chair might have been borrowed from some little girl's dollhouse. She said something then that made the others laugh but the kid couldn't make out her words. Her voice reminded him of a man he had met once in a bar in Kitchener. His voice box had been removed because of cancer and he had a stainless steel gizmo put in there that enabled him to talk, except the words all sounded to the kid like a jew's-harp.

He tried to avoid staring at Maxine but was always aware of her on his left. She sat in a lawn chair in front of the trailer, her hair a flaming metallic red against the dark doorway yawning behind her. The neckline of her loose-fitting blouse gave only a hint of the largest bust the kid had ever imagined possible.

"Any of you notice the same rube the last couple of towns?" Jolly Velma asked.

"A one-man travelling fan club, eh?" Maxine said.

"I have that every now and then, some character following me from place to place. Receive offers from some of them too, I'll have you know," Jolly Velma said, primping her hair, eyelids fluttering.

"He'd try anything with me," Maxine said, "and he'd get a knee in the family jewels."

"The thing is," Jolly Velma said, "he never looks at me, he just sits there lookin' pained, like he's expecting the end of the world or something."

"Admit it, Velma, **that's** really what's bothering you," Amos said, reaching for another Coca-Cola case nearby. He set it upside down in front of him, took out a deck of cards from his back pocket, and began shuffling them, the cards sounding *braaap, braaap* against the wood bottom. He laid them out for solitaire, a dragon on one biceps and a serpent on the other wriggling with the movement of his muscles. On his arms were a heart pierced with an arrow, an open Bible, a bride, and an array of snarling animals: eagles, tigers, and hawks. The kid's favourite tattoo was the one on Amos's left chest; it showed a door with four rectangular panels in it, their corners all filled with fancy curlicues, so that the gold ring hung down from his nipple like a miniature door-knocker. Beside the door stood a majestic lion with paw raised, as if it might at any moment take hold of the ring. The kid wondered where under Amos's shorts the tattoos stopped and where they resumed. "How many you figure you got in all, Amos?" he asked.

"Not enough. Aces are comin' out too slow."

"Tattoos, I meant."

Amos looked at him then the way his father always had whenever he'd said something stupid. "Kid," Amos said, "never pry into a performer's specialty. It destroys the—mystique. Take yourself now. Does anyone here ask you where you're runnin' from?"

"Who says I'm runnin'?"

"I am, cuz it's written all over your face, plain as a tattoo." He shuffled the cards several times, then said, "Nope, the only one flaunting figures around here's Maxine. Ain't that right, Max."

Maxine spread a slow smile across her face, as if she were holding a royal flush to Amos's four aces and knew it. "What's the matter, Amos," she said, preening her bodice, "my little ol' 63 inches too much for you to handle?"

"See what I mean kid?" Amos said.

II

The kid had left home early that summer, after he'd decided that Pastor Levi was carrying things too far. Since high school he'd been working in his father's salvage yard just outside Listowel, where his father had given him a proper Christian upbringing, applying somewhat the same principle in raising his children as he did in growing saplings in the yard: he bound them between stakes to make sure they would grow upright. Every Sunday the family attended Calvary Baptist.

Levi Owens was the pastor there, a lanky man with hair tucked in behind his ears, long blond hair that just failed to cover a huge purple scar on his forehead. He wore a pair of gold-rimmed glasses that made the pupils of his eyes appear sharp as the tines of a pitchfork.

He was a man surrounded by rumour. Some people said he had once been a minor league pitcher out west, others said a professional boxer, still others said they'd heard he was involved with gambling. Pastor Levi himself wouldn't say very much about it, only that he'd been living the life of an unregenerate sinner, until he was converted at a tent revival and he'd turned to preaching.

The Sunday before the kid left, Carol Ann Sheehy had been baptized. Pastor Levi stood behind the pulpit wearing his black suit as usual, despite the heat, the coat hanging on him like a stiff piece of cardboard, sweat matting the hair on his brow.

"We're here to witness the most important event in a Christian's life," he said, "the moment when a child of God has the courage to say 'O God, without your help I'd be lost.' Now I want to talk to you about that, brothers and sisters, especially you younger people who think that you've got all the time in the world before you face up to your spiritual responsibilities. I know what you're thinking, because I wandered myself at one time, moving from place to place with no concern for how I was offending the Lord with my sinful ways, but Jesus the Good Shepherd saw me and took compassion, saw how I'd wandered so far from home I'd never be able to find my own way back, so He left the ninety and nine and came and sought me. 'Brother Levi,' he told me, 'I've come to take you home.' But I'm here to tell you today that the next time Christ comes it may not be in compassion but in **judgement**. It may not be to take you home as one of his sheep, but to separate you as one of the goats. Take heed, therefore!" and here he took out a white handkerchief and wiped his forehead, the deep scar bright purple on his brow and Pastor Levi wiping it as if the scar were a bit of makeup he could rub off if he only tried.

After the sermon he took off his coat, rolled up his sleeves, slowly, as if in ritual preparation for the baptism, then moved beside Carol Ann Sheehy standing in the water in a white dress and, with a strong push on her shoulders, he dunked her backwards into the water, Carol Ann Sheehy coming up again with water streaming from her drenched white dress and her face and her long blond hair.

For three years now, since the kid had graduated from high school, Pastor Levi had been after him to be baptized, telling him he was running away from a decision he'd **have** to make sooner or later, and that it might just as well be sooner. "Don't play around with it, son," he'd said, "don't quench the promptings of the Spirit."

The kid had put him off repeatedly. "There's things and places I ain't seen yet," he said, "and I aim to see them first. I'll tell you when I'm good and ready."

Pastor Levi had impaled the kid with his pitchfork eyes. "Ready or not," he said, "I'll be there."

The carnival had arrived in town on Monday and by Saturday, after spending all week in the salvage yard skinning his knuckles removing usable parts from cars, the kid felt ready to cut loose. Late that afternoon he quit work, ate supper, showered and dressed, then picked up Martin Kooima who lived on the farm next to the salvage yard. Martin's family had immigrated to the area from Holland after the War, and now went to the church attended by all the Dutch people around Listowel. The kid thought they were good people, generally, although they believed some funny things, most of them directly opposite from what the Baptists believed. The kid had talked about it now and then with Martin, complaining that Pastor Levi was hounding him to be baptized.

"I don't know much about it," Martin said. "We all get baptized when we're born, not like you, and even then we just get sprinkled."

The kid's father had told him that that wasn't a legitimate baptism, it had to be total immersion or nothing. But then, the kid thought, the Dutch believed some funny things anyway, so that Martin might not be of too much help here. His people considered it all right to drink and smoke, things the Baptists thought were taboo, but were not allowed to go swimming or anything else on Sunday, which the Baptists thought perfectly fine, except Martin did it anyway. Martin also said they believed in irresistible grace, which meant, he said, that if a person had been chosen by God there was nothing he could do to avoid being saved, God would get him somehow, no matter what. The kid told Martin the Baptists did not believe in irresistible grace but that every person had to decide for himself.

"Aw, that's just Arminian," Martin said, "and you know the old saying: 'where there's a will there's an Arminian,'" but the kid didn't see anything funny in that.

They drove to the fairgrounds and saw all the brightly coloured tents and booths, then as they got closer and had parked the car they could smell the inevitable carnival smells: cotton candy, popcorn, hot dogs, and sauerkraut. Once they were inside they hit the midway

first. Martin won a twisted Seven-Up bottle tossing a quarter onto a
dish and the kid won a turquoise poodle ringing the bell at the
Mighty Mallet. They threw baseballs at milk bottles, basketballs
into peach baskets, footballs through rubber tires. Then they came
to a red and blue striped booth and when they moved closer saw a
large box inside with slots numbered 1 to 13. The betting counter
had squares painted on it labelled *Under 7*, *Over 7*, and *7*, which
paid 3-1. Bettors took turns rolling a large rubber ball until it came
to rest in one of the slots. The operator was a man with black hair
and a green visor shielding his eyes and he jabbered into a microphone
dangling from his neck, his voice hoarse as if he smoked too much.
"Try your luck, folks," he kept saying, "try your luck. Place your
bets and win, nothin to it here." Martin and the kid hung at the edge
of the crowd a while, watching to see how the game worked, then
moved on. They had walked all the way past the Scrambler, the
Screamin' Tornado, the Loop-the-Loop and the Octopus and were
almost to the freak shows before the idea suddenly came to the kid
and he knew it had to be foolproof.

"Hey Martin," he said, "something that's a sure fire thing ain't
gambling, right?"

"I suppose. Why?"

"You know that Under 7 Over 7 game we were at? I just figured
out a way to work it. Can't lose."

"How?"

"What you do is take either Under 7 or Over 7, doesn't matter
which, but whatever one you choose, stick with it. Every time you
lose, double your bet until you win and presto! you make whatever
you started out betting."

"What if you don't win?"

"You've got to. You've got almost a 50-50 chance on every
throw. See what I mean? Figure it out."

"I don't know. You try it first, I'll watch."

They walked back to the red and blue booth and the kid tried
several games in his head. It worked, he was sure of it. He inched his
way to the betting counter.

"That's right boys, step right in and place your bets," the operator
croaked. He handed the kid the ball. The kid placed a quarter on
Under 7, rolled the ball, and it landed on 3. The operator dropped a
quarter by his. "Everybody wins," he said. The kid put the quarter
in his left hand and placed the original quarter back on Under 7. The
ball landed on 8 and the operator slid the quarter into his canvas
apron, a motion so smooth and professional the kid was impressed
by the cleanness of it. This was a place he could take to. He put two

quarters on the counter and this time the ball landed on 7. Several people whooped. "All right folks, some big winners here," the operator said in his gravel voice. The kid began to wonder if his method were foolproof after all as he dug into his wallet for a dollar bill. He placed it on Under 7 again. The ball rolled and landed on 4 and the operator dropped a dollar bill by his. He stuck the two bills into his wallet and hastily did some arithmetic just to make sure he hadn't made a mistake. Amount bet: $1.75. Amount received: $2.00. Profit: yep, 25 cents. He turned back to Martin, smiled, and nudged him in the ribs. "C'mon," he said, but Martin shook his head.

He continued playing a while with quarters, winning slowly until he had a little stack of them hard in his hand. His palm felt clammy and he shifted the quarters into his pocket. Then he thought, why play with quarters, why not go higher, and he raised his starting bet to a dollar. The operator gave him a look from under his green visor, never interrupting the hoarse flow of words from deep in his throat. Some bettors left and new ones took their place. The kid bet a dollar on Under 7. The ball landed on 11 and his dollar was whisked away. He put down two dollars and the ball rolled, landing on 9. He put down four dollars. "Here y'are, big spender," the operator said and handed him the ball. He felt his chest pounding now as he threw the ball into the box. It bounced and landed on 7. "No winners this time," the operator said as he glided behind the counter sweeping money into his apron. The kid had to reach into his wallet again, took out a five and three ones and laid them on the counter. The ball was handed to the man next to him, who looked at the little pile of crumpled bills in front of the kid. The kid felt the eyes of the whole crowd on him. The ball rolled, teetered a moment on 2, then came to rest on 12. "Sorry bud," the man next to him said, shrugging his shoulders, and the kid's money was whisked away. He turned back to Martin. "Lend me a ten."

"You sure?"

"Course I'm sure. I **gotta** keep going now."

Martin handed him a ten. He placed a five and a one beside it and wiped the sweat beading his upper lip. He smelled money on his hands. The operator handed him the ball. "C'mon gov'nor, one more time," he said. The kid took the ball, waited a moment as if to pick out the slot he wanted it to land in, then threw the ball into the box. He watched the ball roll, hovering on 2, then on 9, finally stopping on 1. He felt too relieved to holler but heard Martin whoop behind him.

The operator came over like an alligator gliding through water.

"Whatta we got here," he said, counting the bills. "What, sixteen dollars? You crazy, kid? Sorry but I can't do it. Ten buck limit." He threw the money back on the counter and began to walk away.

"Hey!" the kid shouted after him, "where's it say that? Where's it say ten buck limit? You owe me sixteen bucks!"

The operator turned around, hands spread benevolently, face bland with false regret. "Sorry kid, can't do it. Police ordinance. Ten buck limit, 's nothin' else I can do."

"Well how come you don't tell people that! I don't see it posted anywhere."

The operator came over then and covered the microphone with his hand. "Kid," he said, "how old are ya. Lemme tell ya somethin'," and his voice became condescending, as if he might be a father giving his son some advice. "Next time don't bet more 'n you can afford to lose, huh, so why'ntja call it a day. I got a business to run here and there ain't no use makin' trouble." Then he turned around facing the crowd and his gravelly voice started up again. "Step right up folks, try your luck, nothin' to it here."

The kid walked away, Martin at his side. They wandered the rest of the midway, no heart left to see even Maxine The World's Most Abundant Girl, and drove to the King Edward Hotel where they computed the kid's loss, Martin consoling him with rounds of Molson Golden.

They didn't come home until late in the night, the kid inching his car up the salvage yard's gravel driveway, then coaxing the door shut. Same with the back screen door. He tiptoed across the kitchen linoleum to his bedroom, waiting a moment behind the door to see if his father had awakened, but he heard nothing.

Next morning he slept late, paying no heed to his mother's calls for breakfast. By the time he finally did get up, the family was almost ready to leave for church. His father faced him in the kitchen, face and arms dark with tan, forehead white and his hair rising like the comb of a rooster.

"Where ya been last night," he demanded.

"Out with Martin."

"I said where ya been."

The kid felt too resigned to lie, and he told him he'd been to the carnival. His father looked at him sharply but said nothing, as if he'd expected a lie and was taken aback now by the truth.

"Just so's you didn't shame yourself," he said finally, wagging his finger. "Just so's you didn't commit wickedness."

The kid waited for the others to leave for church before he did. As he pulled out of the driveway his father's blue International was just up the road, raising a cloud of dust that had barely settled by the time he reached it, the dust entering his car without his being able to see it but making the car smell like the inside of an old shed. When he got to town he could taste the dust dry and gritty in his mouth. Just before the fairgrounds he caught up to the pickup and saw his father sitting straight up behind the wheel, looking oddly formal as he always did wearing a Sunday hat instead of his brown visored cap, saw his mother sitting by the opposite door in her white polka dot dress and his younger brother and sister between them, Nancy with a white ribbon in her hair and Tommy in a white shirt and his hair all slicked down with water and Brylcreem.

As he drove past the fairgrounds he noticed that the tents and booths of the carnival were being torn down. He slowed his car until his father's pickup was out of sight, then he turned in just for a look. Three men were rolling huge sheets of canvas, obeying orders shouted at them by a roly-poly man in a wrinkled brown suit. They were obviously a man short, and one of the men had to keep running back and forth between corners. The kid strolled over and watched. "Hey," he said finally to the man in the wrinkled brown suit, "looks like you need another man." The roly-poly man looked at him as if to say who do you think you are, but it was obvious the kid was right. The man looked at him again, then said, "All right, help out with that tarp over there," and the kid jumped to it, his Sunday clothes soon soiled by dirt and grease.

For an hour he helped roll canvas and load it along with innumerable metal bars onto trucks, and he wondered whether his parents would notice him missing from Calvary Baptist. Pastor Levi would be preaching, wearing his black suit as usual despite the heat, the coat hanging on his lanky frame like a stiff piece of cardboard.

He was just starting to get thirsty when the roly-poly man came by again. "You're a good worker, son," he said. "My name's Bustad. What kind of work do you do?"

"I'm a mechanic, I can do carpentry, lots of things."

"O.K., son, you're on," Bustad said.

That same morning, before his family came back from church, the kid drove home, hurriedly packed a suitcase, and slipped out of town with the carnival.

III

Jolly Velma was first to stir. "Guess I'll get me a little something to eat," she said, pushing down on her seat with two chubby hands and labouring to raise the rest of her body. She stood a moment recovering from the effort, then waddled to the steps of her trailer and ascended them one foot ahead of the other like a child climbing stairs. The specially large opening of her trailer looked wide enough for a Volkswagen but her body filled most of it as she walked through.

"Yep, time for a little anti-freeze," Rufus said, and sauntered off.

"And I have a little makeup job ahead of me," Maxine sang, brushing her slacks. She rose from her lawn chair. "Time to get ready for the natives, right Amos?"

"You and me, babe," Amos said. The kid looked at Maxine's feet as she walked by. Then Jolly Velma appeared in the doorway of her trailer, eating a lemon meringue pie.

As it turned out, Bustad had him working the Octopus as usual. The ride's levers were right by the engine, which roared in his ears, competing with the screeching wheels of the Screamin' Tornado and the steady shriek of children's voices everywhere. And it was hot. He'd taken off his shirt long ago, the sun baking his shoulders, while his undershorts crawled up steadily, clinging to his skin, a chafing rash beginning to develop in an awkward spot. He saw himself knocking on Maxine's door. Say, Maxine, I've got this little problem and I was wondering if you might have some Vaseline I could borrow? Sure honey, I know all about it. Come on in.

Across from the Octopus stood the dunking machine. Between rides the kid could hear Rufus's voice taunting the customers over a microphone. Rufus was good at it, usually got the thrower so riled up his aim would be all wild, but every now and then came the *bing!* of the ball hitting the target and the stool collapsing with a squeak that made the kid want to go over there and oil it, and the crowd cheering as Rufus hit the water. The kid sat down and closed his eyes to the cars whizzing all around him. He was now at the point where he could come to within several seconds of three minutes exactly without having to look at his watch. He prided himself on it. He pushed the lever to stop the ride and the kids got off, staggering exaggeratedly, while new ones scrambled to take their place.

Off to the right a barker began drumming up customers for Maxine's next show: "Never before in your life have you seen something like this, folks, you have to see it to believe it. Come on in and . . . " The kid had heard the spiel so often he had the whole thing memorized. Over the cars scrambling back and forth he could see the canvas sheets that advertised the freak show, paintings of Jolly Velma and Amos and Septima and all the rest, paintings that looked nothing like them. He envied them all being able to sit in the shade.

Late in the afternoon a large crowd gathered around the dunking machine, obstructing the kid's view. He heard the *bing*! of the machine regularly, followed every time by a roar from the crowd. Rufus's voice came through the noise, not his usual voice, but with an edge to it. Then the crowd dispersed and Rufus did not appear for the rest of the afternoon.

The kid asked Amos about it at messtime. "I guess some hotshot was giving him a dunking and Rufus'd nipped enough to holler something at him. Bustad let him go."

Next day the dunking machine stood deserted, as quiet as a roadside chapel. The kid looked at it all day from the Octopus, and gradually the idea came to him. He would ask Bustad about it.

He knocked on the boss's trailer door that evening, and a low voice inside ordered him to come in. Bustad was flipping through some papers, hardly aware of the kid.

"Mr. Bustad," he said, "I'd like to ask you something."

Bustad still did not look up. "Go ahead and ask."

"Mr. Bustad, I'd like to become your dunking machine clown."

"Naw, I don't think so, son, that's a highly specialized job."

"But I've been watching Rufus for two weeks now, and I know all the tricks. I'm serious, Mr. Bustad. You can get anybody to run the Octopus, but not the dunking machine. Besides, the carnival needs it."

Bustad looked up, scratching his jowls. "I know, son, but . . . "

"Let me try. You've got nothing to lose."

Bustad looked at the kid again, appraising him as though he might have been a suit of clothes on a rack for sale. "We'll see tomorrow," he said.

The kid knew that he had it.

Next day came hot again as he walked over to the trailer where Bustad was to help him with the clown outfit, and he kept thinking how nice it would be to get cooled off regularly while working, but when he got to the trailer and saw what he all had to wear he thought Bustad had to be kidding. Lying on the table was a pile of thermal underwear, a rubber suit, and the clown outfit.

"All that?" he said.

"I don't know if we should go through with this," Bustad said. But the kid started taking off his clothes before the boss could make up his mind. The thermal underwear and the rubber suit fit fine. "You'll be grateful for them, believe me," Bustad said. "That's unheated water in that tank." He helped the kid put on the clown outfit and the big red and white polka dotted bow tie. Then he began smearing makeup on the kid's face. When he was done the kid looked at himself in the mirror, hardly recognizing himself: red cheeks, a red nose, and an evil-grinning mouth. The makeup felt strange on his face, like an extra layer of skin. On his head Bustad had placed a red cap, two devil's horns protruding from his forehead.

"Listen now," Bustad said, "the secret of this thing is you have to draw a crowd, son. Always be thinking up there. **You're** the one that picks out the next mark. Remember that he won't come to the counter unless you make him. He's there waiting for ya, but you gotta bring him in. If you're any good at it there oughta be somebody throwin' practically all the time, like it's got its own momentum, and the better you are at insulting the mark the less you get wet. But I don't want nothin' dirty, understand, keep it in good taste. All right, let's go and have a look."

Walking to the dunking machine the kid felt like a deep sea diver. He felt that now he was truly part of the carnival—dunking machine clown, Bozo, dealer in insult and revenge.

Bustad stood by the target while he climbed the ladder to the stool. The first thing he noticed when he sat down was that the six feet between the stool and the water was a lot farther than he had thought. Then, as he sat there contemplating the distance, the stool suddenly collapsed beneath him with a squeak.

It took what seemed like a long time before he hit the water. And that water was **cold**, a lot colder than he'd expected. He went all the way under and came up sputtering.

"I wanted you to know what it was like so it wouldn't come as a surprise the first time," Bustad said.

"Thanks, that was considerate."

"You sure you want to go through with this, son?"

He waved at Bustad as he climbed back up to the stool.

"O.K., in fifteen minutes we open."

The job turned out to be much harder than he had thought. The constant chatter gave him a hoarse throat, and the repeated dunking made him feel as if he were in training for some future event. Within a week or two, however, he began learning how to draw a crowd, how to pick out a man and bring him to the counter as if he were a marionette and all the kid had to do was pull the right string. Once he got him there he learned how to insult him with a guttural snarl that so unnerved the thrower that his chances of hitting the target were greatly diminished. He learned how to spot the embarrassing detail: fatness, an ugly facial feature, an odd item of clothing. And if none stood out, he created one—imagined job, girlfriend, drinking habit, anything that would rile the customer into a desire for revenge, as if his dignity depended upon his dunking that clown who had insulted him in front of all those people.

At first the kid worked from what he remembered of Rufus's store of insults, then added his own. He felt that that was, above all, the magic of it, he from his untouchable holy of holies hurling the perfect insult that would keep the crowd laughing and the customer coming back for more.

One day he kept a fellow throwing for a good half hour. He'd seen the group approaching, four fellows wearing oil-stained jeans and no shirts beneath blue denim jackets that had the sleeves cut off at the shoulders to show their tanned and muscled arms. Each of them had a picture of a snarling tiger stitched on the back of his jacket, each wore sunglasses with mirror lenses. They hung back at the edge of the crowd at first, hooting whenever the kid got dunked. He knew they'd be his next customers. "Hey, who have we got over there," he shouted at them. "Looks like some representatives from the local YMCA! C'mon, tough guys, show your stuff!"

The four fellows looked at each other, nodded their heads as if this were some secret signal, and moved forward to the counter. The first one laid his money down. He was the biggest of the four and obviously felt he had the right to be the first to dunk the kid. He threw a ball and missed.

"Aww," the kid hollered, "widdle boy missed the tar-gut. Try again, Tiger!" The crowd laughed and Tiger missed with the next two balls, the crowd needling him all the while.

Then the next fellow pushed his way in. "Hey Clyde!" the kid shouted. "You got oats growin' outa your belly button." The crowd laughed again but Clyde kept his cool and dunked the kid on the third ball. "What's that you were sayin', you mother!" Clyde hollered as the kid climbed out of the water, and his friends all laughed. The next two took their turns and each managed to hit the target once.

So Tiger, who missed all his throws, felt he had something to prove and shouldered his way back in.

"Ho ho," the kid hollered when Tiger laid down his money, "there better be lots more where that came from, cuz you're gonna need it before you see **me** get dunked." Tiger reared back and fired, but the ball sailed into the canvas sheet behind the target.

"Hey ugly face!" the kid shouted, "you look about as bad as you throw." Tiger waited a moment before throwing again in order to collect himself, but when he threw he threw hard, as if sheer velocity was what triggered the target. The ball flew high.

"One more chance, Tiger, then you better let some of your friends try. The boss is liable to think I'm loafin' on the job!" Tiger threw and missed again.

This time he didn't put down a quarter for three balls, he laid down a dollar. The kid's voice found a groove, needling Tiger, needling him. "Hey, guess who's gonna have a sore arm tomorrow. C'mon Tiger, do it, do it to me now!" But Tiger was losing control of himself, no way he was going to hit the target now except for a lucky shot, and he fired the balls one after another as if it were a speed contest, and one after the other the balls sailed by the target, hitting the canvas with a thud.

A large crowd had collected, cheering loudly whenever Tiger missed. "Hey Tiger," the kid shouted, "you throw like a pussycat!" Tiger looked at the kid as if some deep and cherished part of him had been insulted. He took one of the balls, and instead of throwing it at the target, he threw it directly at the kid as hard as he could. The ball bounced off the wire screen protecting the stool, and the crowd jeered. The kid looked around for some police. No telling what Tiger might do next.

It was at that moment the kid saw a man standing at the edge of the roaring crowd, standing so still it seemed he'd stood there waiting all his life with the infinite patience of a suitor, waiting for the kid to ask him to the dunking machine. When the kid looked at him he strode through the crowd to the counter. He removed his black coat, then rolled up his sleeves, slowly, as if it were part of the ritual. A purple scar stood livid on his forehead.

He laid down a quarter, took the three balls Tiger was holding, and laid down two of them, as if he knew one would be all he'd ever need. Then he faced the kid. The crowd had become deathly still.

The rest the kid saw as in a blur. The man twirled the ball several times in his hand as if to get the feel of it, trained his pitchfork eyes on the kid, and the kid knew it was all up. For the first time he felt completely at a loss for insults, as if his whole repertoire had been taken from him and all of him had been stripped clean.

The man looked at him. He kicked up his left leg, drew back his arm, and fired. The kid saw the ball come flying towards the target, red laces spinning, then the ball struck the target dead on with a *bing!* that triggered the catch and collapsed the stool away from under him with a squeak.

He felt the water ice cold on his feet and hands and face and he went all the way under. When he came up out of the tank with water streaming from his head he heard the cheers of the crowd roaring in his ears like a host of angels rejoicing and then the man was beside him, pronouncing his name with right hand raised and saying, "In the name of the Father, the Son, and the Holy Ghost. Amen."

A LESSON IN DANCE

Saturday afternoon my wife decides on impulse to bake bread and stands at the kitchen table kneading the dough, pounding it with the heels of her hands, atoning for the lack of strength in her arms by a violent rocking of her torso like an overzealous masseuse, while I watch her, bemused, from a stool at the counter, drinking still one more cup of coffee after my lunch in order to stall having to rake the leaves.

Suddenly Gwen bursts into the kitchen in black leotards, ready for her dance class. "C'mon Mom, I'll be late!"

"Oh, I forgot," my wife says. She raises her flour-blanched hands in the air like a priest about to pronounce a blessing, then blows the hair out of her eyes with a sudden puff of breath. "I guess you'll have to drive her this time," she tells me.

I think of the dance school located all the way across town, of the front yard buried under autumn leaves, and the rake hanging with diminishing patience, it seems every time I pass it, in the garage. But the dough lies heavy on the table, solid and irrefutable. "Let's go," I tell Gwen, and in a moment, like two children on the lam, we are in the car leaving the leaf-filled yard far behind.

The dance school is a former Methodist church, an ancient brick structure which was to have been torn down for urban renewal, but a group of concerned citizens banded together, declared the building a historic landmark, and the church was saved. Then converted. It is now the Mary Wood School of Dance.

This act of salvage strikes me as being entirely just. When I was a boy in a Fraser Valley town my family belonged to a congregation of Dutch-Calvinist immigrants whose first concern had been to find a place of worship. They could not afford to build, and after extensive search the consistory had reported that the cheapest space to rent was the old Dreamland Dance Hall above the local pool hangout, and the congregation was rocked with debate. Some claimed the building was doubly of the devil, upstairs **and** down. "God dwelleth not in a temple made by hands," others said, "and neither does the devil."

Now the Dutch always having respected the authority of Scripture, that argument settled the dispute, and the following Sunday we gathered at the Dreamland for worship. Dominee Dryfhout wore his minister's black robe, preaching the sermon from a platform once used by the stage band, its sides still brightly festooned with pink plywood saxophones and clarinets and trumpets and drums. Against the walls hung the burnt-out neon remains of gaily-shaped musical notes, while high overhead the false ceiling was painted a deep blue and spangled with a galaxy of cut-out stars, and I kept wishing janitor Harmelink would turn on the fluorescents above the ceiling for full effect. Three years we worshipped in the dance hall, its ghostly silence sanctified by the measured strains of Dutch psalms:

> Maar 't vrome volk, in U verheugd,
> Zal huppelen van zielevreugd,
> (But upright folk, made glad in Thee,
> Shall skip and dance with jubilee),

while I tried to imagine what bodies had once twirled there to what gay music. Since then, however, the upright folk have gathered funds to build a new sanctuary while the Dreamland Dance Hall has kept a date with a wrecker's ball. So now, thirty years later, it is only justice that dance has finally evened the score.

Rather than make two long trips across town I decide to stay the duration of my daughter's lesson. We walk up the cement steps and I swing open the huge gothic door, doffing my cap as we enter. Inside, I wonder what it is about churches that make them the buildings we take longest in which to feel at home. Gwen and I tiptoe up the stairs, she in dancer's natural light tread, I out of reverence, yet the wooden steps creak. A smell of dust and old wood hangs in the air and I half expect to be met by some aged Dutch patriarchs come to reprove me for permitting my daughter to participate in dance, modern jazz at that, but no ghosts appear. Gwen runs to the dressing room, formerly the pastor's study, while I take my place in a pew along the back wall. Opposite me the pulpit has been removed and the front wall covered with mirrors so that I can see a small congregation of mothers chattering far away across a double length of floor, staring back at me, the only male. Against the wall to my right girls huddle nervously in groups, and now and then one girl separates from the rest to perform a quick pirouette, like a bird fluttering momentarily from a branch before settling back down. On the wall behind them, hanging between stained glass windows, are large Norman Rockwell prints of freckle-faced girls staring wistfully into dressing room mirrors or standing frozen in ballerina's stance, one slipper-lace dangling loose. Finally the teacher, a thin woman in leotards coloured a nun's black, calls out "All right girls!" and the lesson begins.

The women's chatter does not abate. "So I says to her, I says, don't let him walk all over you like that," the woman on my left, child on her knee, remarks to the woman beside her.

"I know, that's exactly it," her companion replies.

On the floor the girls are doing warm-up exercises to the brisk cadence of piano music tinkling loudly from speakers in the front corners of the room. The teacher sings out in rhythm: "One-two-three, one-two-three, uuuup-and-back. One-two-three, one-two-three, arms-at-the-side." Black and red and blue leotards cover the girls' bodies, slipping up on their buttocks so that two plump, white half-moons show. Some girls wear wool leggings from foot to mid-thigh, the ones with slim figures resembling randy burlesque queens while the bulkier ones look strangely like hockey players without pants.

"Which one's yours?" the woman beside me asks.

"The blond one, second from the right."

"Hmmm, she's pretty," the woman says, expecting me to return the question, I know, but judging from her own figure her daughter is probably a defenceman.

I watch Gwen. Her long blond hair is tied at the sides in twin ponytails, making her look like a small child, but as she skims along the floor her eyes stare in concentration such as I have never seen in her before. Her head tilts to the right, is held still as one arm flows out in front of her in undulating line to her hand, the middle finger drooping like a petal, then she twirls and glides across the floor, swinging her hips ahead of her rhythmically as if to bounce back a series of opponents. She pauses, flings back her head and arms, then patters back to the mirrored wall in a flurry of steps, her left leg a supporting pillar for her body while her right foot is held out perpendicular to the other, toe pointing to the floor, arms raised with fingertips touching to form a perfect bishop's mitre above her head.

Her body is just beginning to develop although at home she has not yet reached the stage of being self-conscious about her body. She will undress in the living room or leave the door unlocked while taking a bath, and when I inadvertently step in, certain then that I have trespassed, she sings out cheerily, "Hi, Dad!" and starts a conversation as nonchalantly as if we were on a stroll. Nor does she show any embarrassment towards me. A month ago I started locking the door when taking a shower, and Gwen would knock and protest, "Oh Dad, do you **have** to lock the door?"

My own father had always been terribly self-conscious of his body, unwilling to be seen even in a bathing suit, and from him I have inherited a certain clumsiness, as if my body were a strange building in which I have never learned to feel at home. But my daughter's naturalness with her body, an intimate with whom she could share her deepest secrets and not feel shame, has taught me again that we are indeed dwellers of sanctuaries.

After a short hour the lesson is over. As we drive home I pull Gwen to me and she looks wonderingly up into my eyes. But even my devotion she accepts with grace.

Hugh Cook

Hugh Cook was born in The Hague in 1942 and immigrated to Canada with his family when he was seven. He earned an M.A. from Simon Fraser University and an M.F.A. from the Writers' Workshop at the University of Iowa. His stories have subsequently been published in many of Canada's leading literary journals. He and his wife and three teenage children presently live in Hamilton, Ontario, where he teaches Englsih at Redeemer College.

DATE DUE

DEC 20 '06	
OCT 4 2007	
NOV 18 2013	

BRODART, CO.   Cat. No. 23-221-003